"Please, Fausto, don't feel guilty on my account. I was a full participant in this." She gestured to the expanse of sand between them. **"You don't need to have any regrets."**

And yet he did. In that moment he felt swamped by them—by his own lack of self-control, by the desire that still coursed through him. By the sure and certain knowledge that he'd hurt a woman he admired and respected, and yet still knew he could never marry.

But why couldn't he?

The question, so unexpected, suddenly seemed obvious. Why shouldn't he marry Liza Benton? Admittedly, she would not be his family's first choice by any stretch. His mother would be disappointed and hurt. His father would never have countenanced such a choice.

He acknowledged she would struggle to fit into his world, both here and even more so in Italy. She was not from one of Lombardy's ancient families, not by any means. Not even close.

Yet he wanted ⟨…⟩ idn't love her, not y⟨…⟩s. She wouldn't ⟨…⟩rse, she was lovely⟨…⟩

And, he realiz⟨…⟩ moment be ca⟨…⟩ child.

Dear Reader,

I fell in love with Jane Austen's *Pride and Prejudice* when I first watched the 1995 BBC adaptation with Colin Firth. I read the book afterward and then watched the program again with my teenage daughters. Whose heart doesn't beat a little faster at the sight of Mr. Darcy's stern countenance? When my editor asked if I'd be willing to write a Harlequin Presents version of this classic, I was beyond thrilled. Mr. Darcy—so cold, so autocratic, so gorgeous and with a steely core of honor—is, in my opinion, the ultimate Presents alpha male and the perfect hero!

Pride and Prejudice is, in some sense, a dryly clever comedy about manners and society, but in order to turn it into a Presents with all the necessary high-stakes emotion, I really needed to dig deeper into the characters. Why is Mr. Darcy—my Fausto Danti—so arrogant? Why is Lizzy Bennet—my Liza Benton—so quick to judge? Exploring the emotions beneath the witty, charming surface of the story was both challenging and fun, and I fell in love with *Pride and Prejudice* all over again, just as I hope you will!

Happy reading!

Kate

Kate Hewitt

PRIDE & THE ITALIAN'S PROPOSAL

ISBN-13: 978-1-335-40396-4

Pride & the Italian's Proposal

Copyright © 2021 by Kate Hewitt

This edition published by arrangement with Harlequin Books S.A.

For questions and comments about the quality of this book,
please contact us at CustomerService@Harlequin.com.

Harlequin Enterprises ULC
22 Adelaide St. West, 40th Floor
Toronto, Ontario M5H 4E3, Canada
www.Harlequin.com

Printed in U.S.A.

After spending three years as a die-hard New Yorker, **Kate Hewitt** now lives in a small village in the English Lake District with her husband, their five children and a golden retriever. In addition to writing intensely emotional stories, she loves reading, baking and playing chess with her son— she has yet to win against him, but she continues to try. Learn more about Kate at kate-hewitt.com.

Books by Kate Hewitt

Harlequin Presents

Claiming My Bride of Convenience
Vows to Save His Crown

Conveniently Wed!

Desert Prince's Stolen Bride

One Night with Consequences

Princess's Nine-Month Secret
Greek's Baby of Redemption

Secret Heirs of Billionaires

The Secret Kept from the Italian
The Italian's Unexpected Baby

Visit the Author Profile page
at Harlequin.com for more titles.

Dedicated to all the *P&P* fans out there—may you find your Mr. Darcy!

CHAPTER ONE

'YOU'LL NEVER GUESS who just walked in!'

Liza Benton looked at her younger sister's flushed face and laughed. 'I'm sure I won't,' she returned with a smile. 'Considering I don't know a single person in this place.' She glanced around the busy bar in Soho, its interior all sleek wood and chrome stools, pounding music and bespoke cocktails. Right now it was full of glamorous people who had a lot more money and fashion sense than she did, and they seemed to be taking delight in showing both off.

Liza had only moved to London from rural Herefordshire six weeks ago and she was still feeling a bit like a Country Mouse to a whole load of sleek Town Mice. But her younger sister Lindsay, visiting for the weekend with their mother Yvonne, was determined to be the belle of whatever ball—or bar—they frequented.

It had been Lindsay who had assured Liza and their older sister Jenna that Rico's was the place to be. 'Everyone who's anyone goes here,' she'd said with a worldly insouciance that belied her seventeen years. Considering she'd hardly ever left their small village in Herefordshire save for a few school trips, Liza wasn't sure how her sister would know such things, but she seemed confident that she did. Of course, Lindsay was confident—perhaps a bit too confident—about everything, including her own youthful charms.

Looking around Rico's now, Liza didn't think it looked all that special, although she acknowledged she didn't know much about these things. She hadn't been to many bars, and hadn't particularly wanted to. Her twenty-three years had been spent helping out with her large family and then getting her degree; socialising or romance hadn't played much part at all, save for one unfortunate episode she had no desire to dwell on.

'So who walked in?' her older sister Jenna asked with a little laugh as Lindsay collapsed breathlessly onto the banquette next to her, determined to maximise the melodrama. Their mother took a sip of her violently coloured cocktail, eyes wide as she waited for her youngest daughter to dish. She loved a bit of gossip as much as Lindsay did.

'Chaz Bingham,' Lindsay announced triumphantly. Liza and Jenna both stared at her blankly but Yvonne nodded and tutted knowingly.

'I saw him in a gossip magazine just last week. He's recently inherited some sort of business, hasn't he? Investments, I think?' Her mother spoke with the same worldly air as her daughter, although she left Herefordshire even less than Lindsay did. All her knowledge was gained from TV chat shows and tabloid magazines, and treated as gospel.

Lindsay shrugged, clearly not caring about such details. 'Something like that. I know he's loaded. Isn't he *gorgeous*?'

Liza met Jenna's laughing gaze as they both silently acknowledged how their younger sister's excited voice carried. The sophisticated occupants of the table next to theirs exchanged looks, and Liza rolled her eyes at Jenna. She'd never had time for snobs, and she'd encountered a few over the years, people who thought her family was a little too different, a little too loud—her lovably eccentric father, her exuberantly over-the-top mother, and the four Benton girls—pretty Jenna, smart Marie, fun Lindsay…and Liza. Liza had no idea what her sobriquet would be. Quiet, perhaps? Normal? *Dull?* She knew she possessed neither Jenna's looks nor Marie's brains, and definitely not Lindsay's vivacity. That had been made apparent to her on more than one occasion, often by well-meaning people, but once…

She really had no desire to dwell on that now, when they were having so much fun and apparently someone exciting had walked into the bar, even if she'd never heard of him.

'Where is he?' their mother asked, her eyes on stalks as she rubbernecked for a glimpse of the mysterious but apparently impressive Chaz Bingham.

'There.' Lindsay pointed towards the entrance of the bar, and Liza muffled a chuckle.

'Shall we make an announcement on the Tannoy system?' she asked wryly, and her sister gave her a blank look.

'Liza, a bar like this isn't going to have a *Tannoy.*'

'Silly me,' she murmured, and Jenna smiled before she suddenly let out a soft, wondering gasp that had Liza curious enough to see who all the fuss was about. She glanced towards the entrance of the bar and her breath caught as her gaze snagged on the man who had just come in. Now that she'd seen him, it was impossible *not* to notice him. Not to feel as if he took up all the space and air in the place.

He was half a head taller than anyone else in the room, with ink-black hair pushed away from a high aristocratic forehead. Steel-grey eyes under hooded brows scanned the room dismissively, a cynical twist to his sculpted mouth that Liza could see all the way from across the room. Cheekbones like blades and a hard chiselled jaw worthy of any of the steamy novels that Lindsay loved to read.

His powerful physique was encased in a snowy-white dress shirt, unbuttoned at the neck to reveal a bronzed, alluring column of throat—how a *neck* could be sexy, Liza had no idea, and yet it was—and narrow black trousers, an outfit that would suit a waiter, and yet such a thought was laughable when it came to this man.

Everything about him exuded power, wealth, influence and, most of all, arrogance. He looked as if he not only owned this bar, but the entire world. Normally Liza hated conceit of any kind—and she had good reason for it—but this combination of blatant sex appeal and innate arrogance was both compelling and disturbing and, unable to make sense of her thoughts, she forced herself to look away.

'Did you see him?' Lindsay demanded, and Liza jerked her head in a nod. How could she *not* have seen him? Even now, looking away, she could still visualise him perfectly—from that twist of his lips to the powerful shrug of his shoulders. He was emblazoned on her mind's eye, which was another disturbing thought. Why had she reacted so viscerally to a stranger?

'Jenna, I think he's noticed you,' Yvonne whispered excitedly, although her whisper was as loud as Lindsay's, especially after two of her fancy cocktails. Jenna smiled and flushed.

Liza glanced up; the dark-haired Adonis wasn't looking anywhere near her sister, but a friendly-looking man with rumpled blond hair and ruddy cheeks was, with obvious interest. *This* was Chaz Bingham? Then who was the other man?

Unthinkingly, she looked for him, only to find herself suddenly speared on his sardonic gaze for a terrible second, his steely eyes blazing into hers and branding her with their knowledge before, indifferently, he looked away.

'He's coming closer!' Lindsay squealed and, turning away from the man who had so casually dismissed her, Liza wished her sister wasn't *quite* so loud.

Amazingly, Chaz really was coming closer to their table. Liza braced herself, wondering if he was going to ask them to lower their voices, or maybe if he could have the chair they'd piled all their coats on, but he did nothing of the kind. He gave Jenna an immensely appealing smile before turning to them all, including them easily in his friendliness.

'I say, may I buy you a drink?'

'Oh…' Jenna was blushing prettily, and Liza smiled at the man's gentlemanly charm, as well as his obvious interest in her beautiful sister. With her long, tumbling blonde hair and vivid blue eyes, not to mention her curvy figure, Jenna had never been without admirers.

Amazingly, her beauty hadn't made her vain in the least; she'd barely had a boyfriend, and she always seemed surprised by the attention she received. Liza, however, was not, and she had never resented her sister's popularity…even when it had caused her pain.

'Yes, *please,*' Lindsay said, elbowing Jenna meaningfully, and the man—Chaz—smiled and took their orders.

'Of all the women in the whole room,' their mother whispered triumphantly when he'd gone to the bar, 'he chose you!'

'Mum, he's just buying me a drink,' Jenna protested, but Liza saw how her gaze tracked Chaz as he headed towards the bar. Her own gaze moved instinctively to the *other* man in the room, a man who created a tingling awareness all through her body even when he wasn't looking at her. He was clearly with Chaz, for he'd joined him at the bar, propping one elbow upon it as he talked to him, his bored, sardonic gaze moving slowly and disinterestedly around the room.

Really, the look on his face was rather ridiculously arrogant, almost a parody of what Liza imagined some lord of the manor would look like as he gazed down upon his peasants. She felt a thorny spike of annoyance pierce her; why did such a good-looking man have to be so *proud*? Looks weren't everything and yet, Liza acknowledged with an inward sigh, in this world they certainly counted for a lot. She'd discovered that to her detriment—plain Liza compared to pretty Jenna for most of her childhood—and when it had mattered.

'When he comes back,' their mother instructed

Jenna, interrupting Liza's thoughts, 'for heaven's sake, invite him to sit down.'

'*Mum*—'

'Of course she's going to invite him to sit down,' Lindsay interjected with a scoffing laugh. 'And if she won't, I will. I tell you, he's *loaded*.'

'I don't think he'll appreciate the invitation quite as much, coming from you,' Liza interjected with a smile, and her sister gave her a fulminating look. Liza reached for her white wine, which only had one sip left in the glass; she'd declined Chaz Bingham's offer of a top-up. Would Chaz sit down with them if he was asked? she wondered. And if he did, would his dark, proud friend join him? Her heart tumbled over at the thought, and she decided she needed to fortify herself with more wine.

'Liza, where are you going?' her mother demanded, pulling on her sleeve. 'Chaz will be coming back any second—'

Already it was Chaz, she thought wryly. He hadn't even introduced himself yet. 'I've decided I want a glass of wine after all,' Liza said, and with her heart fluttering a little she headed towards the bar—and the intriguing man leaning against it.

'Why on earth did you choose this place?' Fausto Danti glanced around the crowded bar with a grimace of distaste. Having arrived in London from Milan only that afternoon, he'd been hoping for a quiet dinner in a discreet and select club with his old university friend, not a booze-up in a bar that looked like it was full of tourists and college students.

Chaz glanced at him, full of good humour as always.

'What, you don't like it?' he queried innocently. Fausto did not dignify his question with a reply. 'You've always been something of a snob, Danti.'

'I prefer to consider myself discerning.'

'You need to loosen up. I've been telling you that since our uni days. And come on.' He nodded meaningfully towards the table with its bevy of squawking women. 'Isn't she the loveliest creature you've ever seen?'

'She's nice enough,' Fausto allowed, because he had to admit the woman Chaz had set eyes on the second they'd walked through the door was really rather beautiful. 'She's the only pretty one among them.'

'I thought her sisters were nice enough.'

'Sisters?' Fausto arched an imperious eyebrow. 'How do you know they're not all just friends?'

Chaz shrugged. 'They all have a similar look about them, and the older one is clearly their mother. Anyway, I intend to get to know them all. And you can do the same.'

Fausto snorted at such an unlikely suggestion. 'I have no desire to do any such thing.'

'What about the one with curly hair?'

'She looked as plain and boring as the other, if not more so,' Fausto replied. He'd barely glanced at any of the women; he had no intention of picking someone up in a place like this, or even picking up someone at all. His stomach tightened with distaste at the thought.

He'd left such pursuits behind him long ago...and for good reason. He was here in England to deal with the fallout of the London office only, and then he was returning to Italy, where his mother was hoping he would soon announce his choice of bride. His stomach tightened again at *that* thought, although he knew there was no question of not fulfilling his duty.

'Oh, come on, Danti,' Chaz insisted. 'Relax, if you can remember how. I know you've been working hard these last few years, but let's have some fun.'

'This is generally not how I amuse myself,' Fausto replied as he took the tumbler of whisky from the bartender with a terse nod of thanks. 'And certainly not with a couple of obnoxious, gold-digging women who look poised to fawn over your every word.' He'd heard the younger one jabber about how much money Chaz had, not even caring who might be listening.

'Fawning over my every word? That's more your style, mate.' Chaz patted him on the arm and Fausto gave him a tight-lipped smile, even as he felt an uncanny frisson of—something—ripple through him, an awareness he didn't understand, but certainly felt.

He turned swiftly, expecting someone to be standing right next to him, but no one was. He scanned the crowded room but saw only the dull mix of middle class Londoners out for an evening of cocktails and fun.

'Come on,' Chaz said as he hoisted the drinks he'd bought for the motley crew of women, including a revolting-looking cocktail that was garnished with a pink umbrella and no less than three maraschino cherries.

With the utmost reluctance, Fausto followed his friend towards the table of eagerly waiting women. The blonde Chaz had set his sights on was indeed attractive, if in a rather simple way. There was no guile in her clear gaze, no depths to discover in her open face.

Yet, Fausto concluded fairly, he would not necessarily consider her looks insipid.

The second sister, who looked to be still in her teens, was all flash and flare, her make-up overdone, her light brown hair pulled into a high, tight ponytail, a tight cropped top emphasising her curvy figure. The look in her eyes was what Fausto could only call avaricious, and his stomach tightened once more in sour anticipation of a most unpleasant evening.

The mother, he saw, was cut from the same cloth as the sister, and dressed in almost as revealing an outfit—but hadn't there been another at the table? Briefly Fausto recalled curly chestnut hair, a pair of glinting hazel eyes. They were no more than vague impressions, but he held the distinct certainty there had been a fourth woman at the table. Where was she?

Chaz set the drinks down with a gentlemanly flourish and, predictably, the pretty blonde stammered an invitation for him to join them, which Chaz did, sliding into the booth next to her. Fausto was left with no choice of seating other than next to the teenager with a lusty look in her eye, and so he coolly informed them he would prefer to stand.

'I'm sure you would,' a voice quipped near his ear, as the woman he realised he'd been looking for walked briskly by and slid into the booth next to her sister. 'To tell the truth, you seem as if you couldn't get out of here fast enough.'

Fausto locked gazes with the hazel eyes he'd recalled, and they were just as glinting as he remembered. Even more so, for right now they were flashing fire at him, and he wondered why on earth this Little Miss Nobody was looking at him with such self-righteous anger.

'I admit this was not my first choice of establishment,' he returned with a long, level look at this slip of a woman who dared to challenge him. Her hair was the colour of chestnuts and tumbled over her shoulders in a riot of corkscrew curls.

Large hazel eyes were framed with lush chocolate-coloured lashes, and her mouth was a ripe cupid's bow. She wore a plain green jumper and jeans and, all in all, Fausto decided after a moment's deliberate perusal, she was nothing remarkable.

The woman raised her eyebrows as he held her gaze, her angry expression turning to something more mocking, and with a disinterest that was not as legitimate as Fausto would have wished, he flicked his gaze away.

Chaz was making introductions and Fausto turned to listen, although he doubted he would ever have the need to address any of these women by name.

'Jenna… Lindsay… Yvonne… Liza.' Chaz looked as delighted as if he'd just done an impressive sum in his head, and Fausto shoved his hands in the pockets of his trousers. So now he knew her name was Liza, not that it mattered.

'And your name?' the mother, Yvonne, trilled. It was obvious she already knew who he was—Chaz graced enough of the gossip rags and society pages, with his pedigree, wealth and cheerful attendance at many social occasions.

'Chaz Bingham, and this is my good friend from university, Fausto Danti. He's here from Milan to head up his family's London office for a few months.'

Fausto gave him a coldly quelling look; he did not need these people knowing his business. Chaz smiled back, completely unrepentant as always.

'What do you think of our country, Mr Danti?' the mother asked in a cringingly girlish voice. Fausto gave her a repressive look.

'I find it as well as I did when I was here for university fifteen years ago,' he answered coolly, and she gave an uncertain laugh and then blushed, before gulping down her ridiculous cocktail.

Instinctively, unwillingly, Fausto glanced at the woman—Liza—and saw she was glaring at him with unbridled fury. This time she was the one to look away, a deliberate snub which he found both irritating and unsettling. It wasn't as if he *cared*.

Chaz was chatting animatedly to Jenna, which left the four of them—Fausto and these three tedious women—to sit through an insufferable silence. At the start Lindsay attempted a few flirtatious forays of conversation which Fausto shot down unreservedly. He was tired, out of sorts, and he had absolutely no interest in getting to know these people, not to mention a seven a.m. start tomorrow. After fifteen excruciating minutes, he looked pointedly at his watch. Chaz caught his eye and then blithely ignored him. Fausto ground his teeth.

He didn't want to be here, but neither did he wish to be unapologetically rude and leave his friend flat—although perhaps that was what Chaz wanted, all things considered. Fausto glanced at his watch again, even more pointedly this time.

'I'm so sorry we're keeping you,' Liza remarked acidly, and Fausto glanced at her, unperturbed.

'Actually, Chaz is keeping me,' he returned, and she let out a huff of indignation.

'He seems like he's having a good time,' she said with a nod towards Chaz and Jenna, their heads bent together. 'I'm sure he wouldn't mind if you chose to leave.' Her eyebrows lifted and Fausto saw a definite spark of challenge in her eyes that caused a ripple of reluctant admiration to pass through him. Here was a woman with a bit more fire than her beautiful sister, a few more depths to discover. Not that it mattered even remotely to him.

'I'm inclined to agree with you,' he replied with a short nod. 'And so, in that case, I will make my good-byes.' He gave another nod, this one of farewell, his impassive glance taking in all three women before he nodded at Chaz, who gave him a shamefaced grin and kept talking to Jenna.

Fausto couldn't keep from giving Liza one last glance before he left, and as their eyes met something shuddered through him—and then, as dismissive as he had been at the start, she looked away.

CHAPTER TWO

LIZA STARED AT her bedroom ceiling as the autumn sunlight filtered through the curtains and lit her tiny room with gold. She didn't take any notice of it, however, because in her mind she was picturing Fausto Danti, with his steel-grey eyes and his sculpted mouth, his midnight hair and his disdainful look.

Jerk. Rude, arrogant, irritating *boor*.

Her fists clenched on the duvet as she remembered his aristocratic drawl. '*She looked as plain and boring as the other, if not more so.*' She'd heard his damning statement, so indifferently given, when she'd gone to the bar, and the words had scorched through her, branding her with their carelessly cruel indictment. Reminding her that she wasn't anything special—something she'd always felt, had been told to her by someone she'd thought she'd cared about, but to have it confirmed so ruthlessly, and by a *stranger*...

It felt as if Fausto Danti had ripped off the barely healed scab covering the wound she'd done her best to hide from everyone, even herself. She'd always known she wasn't beautiful like Jenna, or intelligent like Marie, or spirited like Lindsay. But to have it confirmed *again*...

After Fausto's callous comment, Liza had raced back to her table, furious and hurt, before he could see her. It wasn't as if she cared or even knew the man, she told herself, and he obviously didn't care at all. The way he'd looked down his nose at them all...as if they were so uninteresting that he simply couldn't be bothered even to make the most basic of pleasantries for a few minutes.

And the way he'd looked at *her*... Liza's fists clenched harder and her stomach did too. There had been something simmering in his iron-coloured eyes that had made everything in her seem to both shiver and heat. As much as she wanted to hate him, and she did, of *course* she did, that look had created a sweet, surprising longing in her she couldn't deny even as she strived to, because she knew it couldn't lead to anything good.

Yet, based on what he'd said, she'd obviously misread that look completely, which added another humiliation to the whole sorry story. Of course he hadn't looked at her like *that*. She wouldn't even know what *that* kind of look was like. She had certainly misread one before.

As for her own humiliating reaction, all heat and awareness...so the man was attractive. Any woman with a pulse would respond to his looks, that much was certain, although after Chaz had left, having exchanged mobile numbers with Jenna, the excited chatter between her mother and sisters had all been about him rather than Fausto Danti.

Would he call? Would he ask Jenna out? When? Where? The deliberations had gone on for half the night, until Liza had finally retreated to bed, unable to contribute to the excitement but not wanting to lower the mood.

She had no doubt that all the conversation today would continue to be about Chaz. No one had even mentioned Fausto Danti last night, which seemed rather incredible considering both his undeniably good looks as well as his undeniably bad manners. But no, her mother and sisters had only wanted to talk about Chaz. Handsome, polite, perfectly nice Chaz Bingham, who was clearly halfway to being head over heels in love with Jenna. And meanwhile Liza couldn't stop thinking about Fausto Danti.

With a sigh she rose from her bed. She had a feeling it was going to be a long day.

By Sunday night, when she said goodbye to her mother and sister who were heading back to Herefordshire, Liza felt it had been a very long two days. They'd shopped on Oxford Street, had tea at The Ritz and seen a West End musical. They'd gone out for curry, strolled through Hyde Park and had makeovers at Selfridge's, and all the while they'd talked of Chaz, Chaz, Chaz.

How rich was he? How many houses did he have? Where had he gone to school? Lindsay had done countless searches on her phone, trumpeting every gleaned fact with triumph while Jenna had murmured something appropriately modest and blushed.

By the end of it all, Liza was heartily tired of even thinking about Chaz Bingham—as well as Fausto Danti. She'd thought about him far too much while her family wittered on about his friend. Why had he been so rude? Who did he think he was? Had she been imagining some sort of…spark…in the look he'd given her? She must have, based on what he'd said to Chaz about her. Of course she had. She was ridiculous to think— *hope*—she hadn't, even for a second. Ridiculous and pathetic.

In any case, they were all futile questions because Liza knew she'd never see him again. In fact, she thought he'd most likely make sure of it, and if he didn't, she would. She *would*.

Still, thoughts of the irritable and inscrutable man dogged her as she headed to work on Monday. Although her position as an assistant to the editor of a tiny, obscure publisher of poetry paid peanuts, Liza loved it.

She loved everything about her job—the elegant, high-ceilinged office in Holborn, with its many bookcases and tall sashed windows overlooking Russell Square. She loved her boss, an elderly man named Henry Burgh, whose grandfather had founded the business a hundred years ago. He was holding onto it now by the skin of his teeth—as well as his generous but dwindling inheritance.

Liza had no idea who bought the slender volumes of poetry with their silky pages and ink-drawn illustrations, but she thought they were the most beautiful books she'd ever seen, and she loved the combination of older canonical poetry with works by refreshingly modern poets.

It annoyed her that as she worked at her desk in that beautiful room, she was *still* thinking about Fausto Danti. Wondering why he was so arrogant—and if there was any chance whatsoever that she might see him again. She really needed to stop.

'You seem a bit distracted,' Henry commented as he came out of his office to give her some manuscripts to copy edit. As usual he was wearing a three-piece suit in Harris tweed, a gold pocket watch on a chain in his waistcoat pocket. For a man nearing eighty, Henry Burgh certainly had style.

'Sorry.' Liza ducked her head in apology. 'Busy weekend. My family visited.'

'Ah, and how did they find the city?' He raised shaggy grey eyebrows as he gave her a kindly smile.

'They loved it, but I knew they would.' Liza thought Lindsay had been waiting all her life to get to London, to the business of living among fashionable people, socialites and YouTubers and the wealthy elite. A school trip to Paris at age twelve was the furthest adventure Lindsay had had so far, and she was most certainly ready for more when she started university next September.

'I'm pleased,' Henry told her. 'The next time they come, you must bring them here to meet me.'

Liza murmured her agreement, although privately she doubted her mother or sisters would want to visit her workplace. None of them, not even Marie, were interested in reading poetry. Her father would, she thought, but he was reluctant to leave the former vicarage in Little Mayton that he'd bought for a song thirty years ago and done up slowly. He loved his home comforts—his study, his workshop, his garden. Unlike his daughters, he had no hankering for adventures outside the home.

What would Fausto Danti think of the place where she worked? Liza wondered after Henry had gone back into his office. Was he a man who liked books? Poetry? Of course she had no idea, and yet somehow she suspected he might. There had been a quiet, contained intensity about him that suggested a man with at least some kind of an inner life, although perhaps that was stupidly wishful thinking on her part. Why should she think the man had depths, just because he had a sexy scowl? No, of course he didn't. He was just a jerk.

Smiling to herself at the thought, Liza reached for the stack of manuscripts.

'Liza!'

Jenna threw open the door of their tiny flat as soon as Liza had reached the top of the stairs, causing her to put her hand to her heart in alarm.

'What's wrong—?'

'Nothing's wrong,' Jenna declared with a chortle. 'Everything is wonderfully right. Or at least—I think it might be! *Look*.' She thrust her phone so close to Liza's face that the screen blurred and she had to take a step back. 'It's from him,' Jenna explained, although Liza had already figured that out.

'If you're free this weekend,' she read, 'I'd love for you to come to a little house party I'm having in Surrey.' She glanced up at Jenna. 'A house party? Really?'

Jenna bit her lip, doubt flickering in her blue eyes. 'Why not?'

'You've met him once, Jen. And now he wants you to go to his house? Doesn't it seem…' Liza struggled for a way to explain her concerns that didn't sound too harsh '…a bit much, a bit too soon?' she finished helplessly.

'There will be loads of other people there. And it's only for the weekend.'

'I know, but…'

'This is what people like him do, Liza. Just because we've never been to house parties doesn't mean it isn't the usual thing.'

'I suppose.' Liza handed back the phone as she headed into their flat. She was tired and her feet ached from her walk from the Tube. She was looking forward to an evening of ice cream and maybe some Netflix, but it was clear her sister wanted to talk about Chaz. Again. Not that she'd begrudge Jenna anything, because her sister was her best friend and just about the most genuinely sweet person in the world. She was the one with the attitude problem.

'Do you think I shouldn't go?' Jenna asked as Liza opened the fridge to peruse its meagre contents. 'I won't if you don't think I should.'

'It's not for me to say…'

'But I need your input,' Jenna protested. 'I trust you, Liza. Do you think it's a crazy idea? I barely know him. It's just he seems so *nice*.'

'He does,' Liza admitted, because that much was certainly true.

'And I do like him.' Jenna bit her lip. 'More than I probably should, considering how little I know him.'

'There's no reason not to go, really,' Liza said as she closed the fridge and started examining the contents of their cupboards. 'We came to London for adventure, after all. Now you're having one.'

'Yes…' Jenna still looked uncertain. The truth, Liza knew, was that her older sister had never been particularly adventurous. It had been more Liza's idea than Jenna's to come to London, desperate for a new start, after she'd been offered the job of editorial assistant. Jenna had found a position as a receptionist at an accountancy firm, and Liza had bowled them both along. It wasn't like her older sister to step out on her own. It never had been. 'I know,' Jenna said suddenly. 'What if you go with me?'

'What?' Liza turned from her disappointing perusal of the cupboards. 'Jenna, I can't just show up without an invitation.'

'I'm sure I could bring a plus one.'

'I'm sure Chaz Bingham is counting on you *not* bringing a plus one,' Liza returned dryly. 'There's no way I can just turn up like a spare part and act as if I was invited.'

'Please, Liza.' Jenna's eyes widened appealingly as she gave Liza a pleading look. 'You know how nervous I get on my own. I'm no good at these kinds of things…'

'We've never *been* to this kind of thing—'

'Parties. Social events. You *know*. I never know what to say, and I go all shy and silent. I need your support.'

Liza shook her head resolutely. 'Jenna, if you're too nervous to go on your own, you shouldn't go at all. You could always go and then leave if you really don't like it. But I cannot, and will not, turn up uninvited.' She suppressed a shudder at the thought. If Chaz Bingham was having a house party, there was a chance Fausto Danti would be there and she could only too well imagine the incredulous and disdainful look on his face if she appeared unexpectedly, an obvious hanger-on. He might think she was trying to attract his attention, *and* she'd be seeming to confirm the unkind remark he'd made about them being gold-diggers. No, thank you!

'I don't know...' Jenna murmured, fiddling with her phone, and Liza reached for a packet of pasta, realising this conversation might take the entire evening and she was going to need sustenance for it.

It took three days of deliberation, but on Thursday morning Jenna finally decided to accept the invitation. Liza helped her word a polite but reserved text back to Chaz.

By Friday afternoon Jenna was packed, and Liza saw her off on the train to Chaz's family estate in Surrey, trying to squelch that treacherous flicker of envy that Jenna was going somewhere exciting and she wasn't. Of course Chaz wouldn't have invited *her*, and Fausto Danti wouldn't have extended an invitation either. The idea was utterly ludicrous; it wouldn't have even crossed his mind, and it was shaming that it had crossed hers, even for an instant.

Besides, Liza reminded herself as she headed back to her flat for a quiet weekend alone, she wouldn't have wanted to go anyway. If either man had invited her, she would have refused. Politely, but most definitely firmly. The last thing she needed was a man in her life making her feel inferior, unwanted. Undesirable.

Although, to be fair, Fausto Danti hadn't been quite that bad. No, she was projecting onto him the feelings she still had about being so thoroughly rejected by Andrew Felton. Liza closed her eyes, determined not to think of the man she'd convinced herself she'd been love with, only to have him laugh at her, and worse.

It had been a long time ago now—well, eighteen months—and she hadn't been that hurt. She hadn't even

loved him, not really, even if at the time she thought
she had.

It was stupid to think of Andrew just because Fausto
Danti had been similarly snide. Fausto Danti, Liza acknowledged, was a million times more attractive—and
therefore a million times less likely to be interested in
her. The sooner she got that through her head, the better.

As one of four sisters, Liza was used to being around
people, but she had never minded her own company
and she would normally be perfectly content to spend
a weekend alone, even if the weather was dire—as cold
and rainy an October as there had ever been.

This weekend, however, the hours seemed to drag
and drag. There were no texts from Jenna even though
she'd promised to tell her how she was getting on and,
with the weather so miserable, Liza decided to stay inside. On Saturday afternoon, with little else to do, she
began to blitz clean the flat; two hours into her efforts,
when she was sweaty and dirty and covered in dust, her
phone finally buzzed with a text from Jenna.

Liza, HELP! I've come down with the worst cold and
everyone here is such a snob. I'm soooo miserable.
Please, please come and rescue me.

'Check.'

Chaz let out a groan as he looked down at the chessboard. 'How did I not even see that?'

'You never see it,' Fausto remarked dryly. 'In all the
times I've played you in chess.'

'Too true. I think we should try another game.'

'Go Fish?' Fausto suggested and Chaz laughed.

'That's about my speed.' He glanced out of the window at the rain streaking relentlessly down the long diamond panes, the view of Netherhall's park shrouded in gloom. 'This weather is horrendous.' He rose from the unfinished game and began to prowl about the elegant confines of the study.

'If you're going to have a house party in October,' Fausto remarked, 'you should expect rain.'

'It's not that.'

Fausto leaned back in his chair as he surveyed his old friend. 'Let me guess,' he said. 'It's the fact that your so-called guest of honour is currently laid up in bed.'

Chaz turned to him with his usual ready smile, eyebrows raised. 'So-called?'

Fausto lifted one shoulder in a negligent shrug. 'Did you *meet* her mother?'

Chaz did not bother to defend the woman in question, which did not surprise Fausto. The woman had been too appalling, with her breathy voice and her avaricious manner, not to mention her revolting cocktails. The same with the younger sister. Gold-diggers, the pair of them, and he certainly knew how to recognise one. Admittedly, he couldn't fault either Liza or Jenna, although he still had his suspicions. A woman could seem sweet on the outside and be thinking only about money and prestige.

Look at Amy...

But he refused to think of Amy.

'So?' Chaz answered with a shrug, drawing Fausto out of his grim recollections. 'I didn't invite her mother.'

'Still, it's telling.'

'Of what?'

Fausto toyed with the queen he'd taken off Chaz a few moments earlier, his long fingers caressing the smooth white marble, memories of Amy still haunting his mind like ghosts. 'They're not exactly people of…class.'

Chaz let out a huff of disbelieving laughter. 'You sound about a hundred years old. This isn't the eighteen-hundreds, Danti.'

It was an accusation Fausto had heard before from his friend. People weren't supposed to talk about class any more, or the fact that someone with a position in society had a duty to uphold it.

But it had been drilled into him since he was a child, by both his parents—ideas about respect, and dignity, and honour. Family was everything, and always came first—above happiness, pleasure, or personal desire. He'd rebelled against it all once, and it had cost both him and his family greatly. He had no desire to do it again.

For a second he saw his father Bernardo's proud and autocratic face, turned haggard and wasted by disease. Fausto could almost feel his father's claw-like fingers scrabbling for his own. *Family, Fausto. Family always comes first. The Dantis have been the first family of Lombardy for three hundred years. Never forget that. Never dishonour it. You carry our name. You represent it everywhere…'*

It was a responsibility he'd shirked once and now took with the utmost seriousness, a burden he was glad to bear, for the sake of his father's memory. It defined who he was, how he acted, what he believed. He would never forget he had a duty to his father, to his family, to himself. A duty to act honourably, to protect the family's interests, to live—and to marry—well, to carry on the Danti name, to run the vast estates that bore his name.

Chaz, he knew, did not feel the same sense of responsibility that he did. His friend wore his wealth and privilege lightly, carelessly, and he did not let himself be weighed down by expectation or tradition—not, Fausto acknowledged, that his parents, currently living in the south of France, cared too much for either. They were new money, a family of socialites, eager to enjoy their wealth. Yet, for all that, Chaz was as friendly and unpretentious a person as any Fausto had ever met.

'In any case, you're not serious about this woman, are you?' he asked.

'I don't know,' Chaz returned thoughtfully. 'I might be.'

Fausto chose not to reply. He couldn't see his friend marrying such a nobody, beautiful though she might be, but if he wanted to amuse himself with an affair, that was his own business.

'Hopefully she'll take some paracetamol then,' he remarked. 'So you can at least see her before she has to go home.' Jenna Benton had shown up at the house late on Friday afternoon, soaking wet and sneezing. She'd barely said a word at dinner, shooting Chaz beseeching looks, and had been holed up in her room ever since.

The other guests Chaz had invited—the usual tedious selection of socialites and trust fund babies—had been as insipid as Fausto had expected. He should have stayed in London and worked through the weekend, but he'd allowed Chaz to convince him to come. Clearly a mistake.

'Perhaps I'll check on her now,' Chaz said, brightening at the thought. 'Make sure she has tea and toast and whatever else she needs.'

'By all means, go and play nursemaid.' Fausto replaced the queen piece on the chessboard before gesturing to the door.

Chaz smiled wryly. 'Are you going to closet yourself in here all weekend? You could have gone into Guildford with everyone else, you know.'

'In the pouring rain?' Fausto shook his head. That afternoon the other three guests had gamely gone into town, but Fausto had refused.

'I know my sister in particular is hoping you'll venture out,' Chaz remarked slyly. 'She was the one to insist you come along.'

'I'm sorry to disappoint her.'

Chaz let out a laugh. 'I don't think you're sorry at all.'

Fausto decided in this case discretion was the better part of valour. As much as he liked Chaz, he had very little patience with his twittering and vapid sister, Kerry. Chaz laughed again, and shook his head.

'All right, suit yourself. I'm going to check on Jenna.'

'Good luck.'

As Chaz headed upstairs, Fausto rose from his chair by the fire and walked about the room, as restless as Chaz had been a moment ago. Perhaps he would make his excuses and return to London tonight.

Danti Investments' London office had been in lamentable shape when he'd arrived last week, a fact which still made him burn with futile fury for its cause. It would take all his time and effort to get it to the productive place it needed to be before he returned to Milan.

He didn't have time to waste enduring the company of people he actively disliked.

For a second an image flitted in his mind of someone he didn't actively dislike…someone he didn't actually *know*. Corkscrew curls, hazel eyes, a mocking smile, a willowy figure. Jenna's sister Liza had been occupying too many of his thoughts since he'd first laid eyes on her last weekend.

It was absurd, because she was of absolutely no importance to him, and yet he kept thinking about her. Remembering the pointed sweetness of her tone as she'd sparred with him, the lively intelligence in her face, the sweetly enticing curves of her slender figure. It was aggravating in the extreme that he kept thinking about her, especially when he had no desire to.

When he married, it would have to be to a woman of appropriate status and connections back in Italy, from one of the ancient families he'd known for many years, who held the same values of honour and respect that he did, who knew how to be his partner in running the vast Danti empire. That had been the promise he'd made to his dying father, and he intended to keep it.

As for other, less honourable, possibilities…he had no desire to get caught up in some run-of-the-mill affair that would undoubtedly run its short and predictable course, and in doing so become messy and time-consuming. Sexual gratification could be delayed. Work—and family—were far more important than such base needs.

The sonorous chimes of the house's doorbell echoed through the hall and Fausto stilled, wondering what unexpected guest might be making such a late appearance.

He waited, but no one came to answer the door; Chaz had to be busy with Jenna, and the staff were no doubt occupied elsewhere. The doorbell rang again.

With a hurried exhalation of annoyance, Fausto strode out of the study. It was most likely only a delivery man or some such, but he hated rudeness or impunctuality, and not answering the door was both.

The large entrance hall was empty as he walked through it, towards the front door. Rain streamed down the windows; it really was a deluge out there. Barely reining in his impatience, Fausto threw open the door with a scowl—and then blinked at the bedraggled figure standing there, looking woebegone and forlorn and very, very wet.

He gaped for a second before his mouth snapped shut and he stared at her, eyebrows creasing together, his mouth drawn down into a disapproving frown.

'Liza Benton,' he stated coolly. 'What on earth are you doing here?'

CHAPTER THREE

Of all the people to answer the door. Liza blinked through the rain streaming down her face at the sight of Fausto Danti glaring at her so predictably. He didn't seem like the kind of man who lowered himself to answer doors, so Liza had no idea why he was standing here before her, looking down his nose at her just as he had before.

What she did know was that she was freezing cold and dripping wet, her clothes sticking to her skin, her hair in rat's tails about her face as she shivered visibly. When she'd answered Jenna's summons and arrived in the village of Hartington by train, she'd been told Netherhall was only five minutes' walk from the station. It was more like fifteen, and thirty seconds after she'd started it had begun to bucket down with rain. So here she was, soaking wet and staring at Fausto Danti. Perfect.

'I'm here to see Jenna,' she said with as much dignity as she could muster, which she feared wasn't all that much. 'She texted me and asked me to come because she wasn't feeling well.' It sounded lame to her own ears. *Why* had she hared off so impetuously after receiving Jenna's text?

She'd grabbed her purse and coat and been at the train station in less than twenty minutes, without a thought or care in the world. It was only now, as Fausto Danti regarded her with such chilly hauteur, that she realised how ridiculous—and possibly scheming—she must seem. It wasn't as if Jenna was at death's door. She had a *cold*. Did Danti think she'd come here for him? Liza squirmed inwardly at the humiliating possibility.

'By all means, come inside,' Fausto said and he stepped aside so Liza could enter, dripping muddy water all over the entrance hall's gleaming parquet floor. She felt entirely at a disadvantage—wet, cold, dirty and, worst of all, uninvited. And all the while Fausto Danti lounged there, his hands in his pockets, his expression one of unveiled incredulous condescension.

'I'm sorry to come unannounced like this,' Liza said stiffly. 'But Jenna sounded completely miserable, and I didn't want her to be alone.'

'She is hardly alone.'

Any other man, Liza reflected, any normal, polite, kind, well-brought-up man at least, would have graciously dismissed her apology and insist that she needn't have made it. He would have ushered her in, offered her a cup of something warm and told her she could stay as long as she liked. She was quite sure that was what Chaz Bingham would have done. Why couldn't *he* have answered the door? Or his blasted butler? Surely he had one.

Anyone but Danti. *Anyone.*

'You are very wet,' Fausto observed.

'It's raining.'

'You didn't take a cab?'

'It wasn't raining when I left the station,' Liza returned with some asperity. 'And I was told it was a five-minute walk. And,' she flung at him for good measure, sensing it would annoy him somehow, 'I'm not in the habit of wasting money on cabs.'

'It would have been five pounds, at most,' her adversary returned mildly, 'but I take your point. Why don't you come into the study? There's a fire in there and you can dry off.'

This unexpected kindness appeased Liza somewhat, but she was still miffed by his high-handed manner and, moreover, stepping into a study with him felt a bit like entering the lion's den without either weapon or armour. Besides, she wanted to see her sister.

'I'm here to see Jenna,' she said, aware that an irritating note of petulance had entered her voice. Fausto raised his eyebrows, his mobile mouth quirking in the smallest of mocking smiles.

'You can hardly see her sopping wet. Besides, Chaz is with her now, and I'm quite sure you don't want to interrupt whatever *tête-à-tête* they might be having.'

Liza frowned at him, trying to gauge his tone. No, she didn't want to interrupt them, but the sharpness in Fausto's voice made her feel uneasy and defensive. What was he implying? Another stupid antiquated reference to gold-digging?

'Very well,' she said, not wanting to pursue the point, and she followed him into a pleasant wood-panelled room where a fire was burning cheerily. Fausto gestured her towards the blaze and as she started towards it, anticipating its wonderful warmth, his hands came to rest on her shoulders.

She stiffened in shock as an electric awareness pulsed through her, starting from the warmth of his hands on her shoulders and racing to every extremity with disturbing force and speed.

'Your coat,' he murmured after an endless unsettling moment, and Liza closed her eyes in mortification. He just wanted her *coat*. What had she been thinking— that he was making a move on her? As if…! Surely she knew better than to think such a thing. She prayed he hadn't noticed her humiliating reaction.

'Thank you,' she muttered, and she shrugged out of the wet garment. She turned, and the sight of Fausto Danti with her battered, sopping jacket in his hands, his expression rather bemused, made her suddenly laugh out loud, that moment of unsettling awareness thankfully dissipated.

He raised his eyebrows in query. 'What's so funny?'

'The sight of you with my poor coat in your hands. It just looks rather…incongruous.'

He glanced down at her coat, five years old and bought off the bargain rack, and then with a shrug draped it over a chair. His hooded gaze swept over her, his face as inscrutable as ever, but all the same Liza was conscious of her very wet clothes; without the protection of her coat, she realised they were clinging rather revealingly to her body, and she plucked uselessly at her sodden jumper.

'You should change,' Fausto said abruptly. 'Did you bring any spare clothes?'

'No,' Liza admitted. 'I—we—won't be staying.'

His eyebrows lifted once more. 'It's already six o'clock in the evening. You can hardly be returning to London tonight.'

Liza shrugged, defensive again. 'Why not? It's not as if we're in the sticks out here. There are trains running to London all the time.'

'Not from Hartington. They stop at four in the afternoon. And in any case I'm sure Chaz won't hear of it. He hasn't spent any time with Jenna yet.'

'If she has a cold…'

'I have no doubt some paracetamol and a bit of TLC will perk her right up,' Fausto replied, his tone so dry that Liza prickled again. Why did he have to sound so cynical? What was he accusing Jenna of—just wanting Chaz for his money? It was an ugly idea, as well as a ludicrous one if he'd spent two minutes with her sister. 'I'll fetch you some clothes,' he stated, and turned towards the door.

'I can borrow Jenna's—' she protested, but Fausto silenced her with a look.

'Nonsense. You can't remotely be the same size.'

Liza blushed at that, for the truth was Jenna was far curvier than she was, as well as a good four inches taller. Still, it annoyed her that Fausto presumed to know their sizes. Before she could make any further protest, however, he was already gone, the door clicking decisively shut behind him and leaving Liza alone in the room.

Restless and edgy, she paced the study, glancing at the leather-bound books lining the walls—all very distinguished tomes—and then at the chessboard set in front of the fire, clearly an unfinished game, with black at a distinct advantage.

She was still studying the board when Fausto returned with a bundle of clothes under his arm.

'Do you play?' he asked, sounding so sceptical that some sudden contrary instinct made Liza widen her eyes innocently.

'Sometimes. Do you?'

He gave a terse nod, and that impish instinct inside her gave voice once more. 'Perhaps you would give me a game?'

Fausto looked startled, and then he thrust the clothes at her. 'Perhaps you should get dressed first.'

'Very well.' Of course he wasn't going to play a game of chess with her. She'd only asked to tease him, which had been stupid of her. Fausto Danti did not seem like a teasing sort of person. Flushing from the humiliating ridiculousness of it all, Liza turned away.

Everything about this situation was so very *odd*, she reflected rather grimly as she took the clothes and Fausto gave her directions to a powder room down the hall. It didn't seem to be much of a house party since the house, enormous as it was, appeared empty.

She found the powder room, which was as big as her flat's living room, without trouble and groaned at the sight of her reflection in the gilt-edged mirror—hair in a frizzy mess, cheeks and nose reddened with cold and the jumper and jeans which had been perfectly respectable when she'd put them on this morning now clinging to her like a second skin. No wonder Fausto Danti had been looking at her so disdainfully.

With a dispirited sigh Liza peeled off the wet clothes

and hung them on the towel rail to dry. Dubiously she inspected the outfit she'd been given—a modest yet clinging dress in cranberry-coloured cashmere.

It slid over her chilled skin as soft as a whisper, making her wonder whose it was. She scrunched her hair and blotted her face, knowing there was little else she could do to repair the damage wrought by the rain. She still looked very much like a drowned rat, if a little less so than before. She supposed it didn't really matter. She could hardly hope to impress him, and she certainly wasn't going to humiliate herself by trying. She knew how that would go.

As Liza headed back to the study, she wondered yet again where everyone was. She felt like Goldilocks stumbling upon a castle rather than a cottage, and instead of three bears there was merely one incredibly intimidating—and attractive—man.

Having no idea what to expect of this encounter, Liza pushed open the door of the study and peeked in. To her surprise, Fausto was sitting at the chessboard in front of the blazing fire. He'd set the board up for a new game, and he gestured to it as she entered the room.

'Well?' His heavy-lidded gaze swept over her figure, clad in the clinging red dress, her feet bare, but he made no further remark. Liza pushed her damp hair away from her face.

'You want to play?' she asked incredulously.

'I believe you asked for a game.'

'So I did.' Her stomach fizzed with sudden expectation and excitement. She hadn't thought Fausto would humour her in such a way, and she had no idea why he was, but as she took her seat across from him she realised in a scorching instant why she'd come all the way to Netherhall in the pouring rain. It hadn't been to rescue her sister, as much as she loved her. It had been to see *him*—the incredibly attractive, arrogant, frustrating and fascinating Fausto Danti.

Fausto studied his opponent from under his lashes as she considered the board. They'd played the first moves in silence, and he'd noted her predictable use of the Spanish Opening, attacking his knight on the third move. Basic but acceptable, and about what he'd expect from someone who played chess but was still a beginner. At least she didn't call the knight a horse.

He was reflecting on whether to put her out of her misery right away or prolong the game simply for the pleasure of seeing her sitting across from him—the dress he'd taken from Chaz's sister's wardrobe fitted her just as he'd hoped it would, skimming her slender curves with an enticing delicacy, making her look warm and so very touchable.

Her legs were bare, slim and golden, one foot tucked up under her, her hair, as it dried from the warmth of the fire, curling up into provocative ringlets about her heart-shaped face. Everything about her was utterly delectable.

Fausto didn't wish to consider what contrary impulse had led him to agree to her suggestion of a match, but he suspected it was a rather base one. The sight of the firelight glinting on her still-damp curls, the pretty flush on her face as well as the gentle rise and fall of her breasts…it was all a distraction he did not need, and yet even so he found he was enjoying it immensely and he could not be sorry.

'I've never been to a house party,' Liza remarked as she unexpectedly—and, Fausto thought, amateurishly—moved her bishop, 'but I always assumed there would be guests involved.' She looked up at him with laughing eyes. 'Where is everybody?'

'They've all gone to Guildford,' he replied as he moved his knight. 'Since they were so bored here, with the rain.'

'Except for Jenna and Chaz?'

'Jenna stayed because of her purported cold, and Chaz stayed because of Jenna.' Fausto spoke tonelessly, refusing to let his own suspicions colour his words, but Liza frowned anyway, her eyes crinkling up as she cocked her head.

'Purported?' she repeated a bit sharply.

'I have not seen her, so I cannot judge for myself.'

'And yet you judge no matter what,' she returned tartly as she flicked her hair over her shoulders and moved her queen. 'Regardless of the situation.'

'I judge on what I see,' Fausto allowed as he captured her queen easily. She looked unfazed by the move, as if she'd expected it, although to Fausto's eye it had seemed a most inexpert choice. 'Doesn't everyone do the same?'

'Some people are more accepting than others.'

'Is that a criticism?'

'You seem cynical,' Liza allowed. 'Of Jenna in particular.'

'I consider myself a realist,' Fausto returned, and she laughed, a crystal-clear sound that seemed to reverberate through him like the ringing of a bell.

'Isn't that what every cynic says?'

'And what are you? An optimist?' He imbued the word with the necessary scepticism.

'No, that's Jenna. I'm the realist. I've learned to be.' For a second she looked bleak, and Fausto realised he was curious.

'And where did you learn that lesson?'

She gave him a pert look, although he still saw a shadow of that unsettling bleakness in her eyes. 'From people such as yourself.' She moved her knight—really, what was she thinking there? 'Your move.'

Fausto's gaze quickly swept the board and he moved a pawn. 'I don't think you know me well enough to have learned such a lesson,' he remarked.

'I've learned it before, and in any case I'm a quick study.' She looked up at him with glinting eyes, a coy smile flirting about her mouth. A mouth Fausto had a sudden, serious urge to kiss. The notion took him so forcefully and unexpectedly that he leaned forward a little over the game, and Liza's eyes widened in response, her breath hitching audibly as surprise flashed across her features.

For a second, no more, the very air between them felt tautened, vibrating with sexual tension and expectation. It would be so very easy to close the space between their mouths. So very easy to taste her sweetness, drink deep from that lovely, luscious well.

Of course he was going to do no such thing. He could never consider a serious relationship with Liza Benton; she was not at all the sort of person he was expected to marry and, in any case, he'd been burned once before, when he'd been led by something so consuming and changeable as desire.

As for a cheap affair…the idea had its tempting merits, but he knew he had neither the time nor inclination to act on it. An affair would be complicated and distracting, a reminder he needed far too much in this moment.

Fausto leaned back, thankfully breaking the tension, and Liza's smile turned cat-like, surprising him. She looked so knowing, as if she'd been party to every thought in his head, which thankfully she hadn't been, and was smugly informing him of that fact.

'Checkmate,' she said softly and, jolted, Fausto stared at her blankly before glancing down at the board.

'That's impossible,' he declared as his gaze moved over the pieces and, with another jolt, he realised it wasn't. She'd put him in checkmate and he hadn't even realised his king had been under threat. He'd indifferently moved a pawn while she'd neatly spun her web. Disbelief warred with a scorching shame as well as a reluctant admiration. All the while he'd assumed she'd been playing an amateurish, inexperienced game, she'd been neatly and slyly laying a trap.

'You *snookered* me.'

Her eyes widened with laughing innocence. 'I did no such thing. You just assumed I wasn't a worthy opponent.' She cocked her head, her gaze turning flirtatious—unless he was imagining that? Feeling it? 'But, of course, you judge on what you see.'

The tension twanged back again, even more electric than before. Slowly, deliberately, Fausto knocked over his king to declare his defeat. The sound of the marble clattering against the board was loud in the stillness of the room, the only other sound their suddenly laboured breathing.

He *had* to kiss her. He would. Fausto leaned forward, his gaze turning sleepy and hooded as he fastened it on her lush mouth. Liza's eyes flared again and she drew an unsteady breath, as loud as a shout in the still, silent room. Then, slowly, deliberately, she leaned forward too, her dress pulling against her body so he could see quite perfectly the outline of her breasts.

There were only a few scant inches between their mouths, hardly any space at all. Fausto could already imagine the feel of her lips against his, the honeyed slide of them, her sweet, breathy surrender as she gave herself up to their kiss. Her eyes fluttered closed. He leaned forward another inch, and then another. Only centimetres between them now…

'Here you are!'

The door to the study flung open hard enough to bang against the wall, and Fausto and Liza sprang apart. Chaz gave them a beaming smile, his arm around a rather woebegone-looking Jenna. Fausto forced a courteous smile back, as both disappointment and a very necessary relief coursed through him.

That had been close. Far, far too close.

CHAPTER FOUR

LIZA'S SENSES WERE still swimming as she blinked her sister and Chaz Bingham into focus. Had that really happened? Had Fausto Danti almost *kissed* her?

She touched her tongue to her lips, as if she could feel the press of his lips against hers still, even though he hadn't actually touched her at all.

She had been able to imagine it so thoroughly, even as she recognised she could not truly envision it at all. In her twenty-three years, Liza had had a handful of casual dates, and one total disaster. None of it had, thankfully, gone too far, although she was still reeling from the emotional fallout of her almost-fling with Andrew Felton, even if she pretended otherwise.

Still, none of her experience, those few kisses, had been as memorable, as mind-blowing, as she was sure Fausto Danti's would be. As even the *possibility* of his had been.

But he hadn't kissed her and, looking at him now standing in front of the fire, his expression as austere as ever, she thought he never would.

She had a sudden, awful certainty that she'd imagined the whole thing; it had been a fabrication of her fevered mind, of the utterly inconvenient longing she'd felt for this man since she'd first stepped into Netherhall. Even now she felt overwhelmed by the height and breadth and power of him, the sight and sound, even the *smell* of him, a sharp, woodsy aftershave that made her senses tingle, along with everything else.

But of course he wasn't interested in her. He couldn't be. Realisation scorched through her. He must have been teasing her, toying with her, and she'd fallen for it completely.

'Liza!' Jenna exclaimed, and started towards her.

Feeling clumsy and stiff, Liza hugged her sister. 'Are you okay?' she asked.

Next to her, Fausto drawled, 'It *was* just a cold, wasn't it?'

Liza threw him a glare that was meant to be mocking. Jenna let out a wobbly laugh.

'I think I've made a fuss over nothing. Chaz gave me some paracetamol and a cup of tea and I feel *so* much better.'

Jenna smiled adoringly at Chaz, who puffed his chest out as if he'd scaled Mount Everest rather than doled out a couple of tablets. Liza could not keep from glancing again at Fausto, whose inscrutable expression still managed to relay his arrogant assurance that he had been entirely correct about the nature of Jenna's *purported* cold, and she fumed inwardly. How could she dislike a man and yet want him to kiss her so much? *So much she'd imagined the chemistry that she'd felt pulsing between them?*

'I'm sorry I made you come all this way,' Jenna said

with a guiltily apologetic look for Liza. 'I was just feeling so low.'

'I'm sure you were,' Liza murmured. She could not deny the awkwardness she felt now at having gate-crashed, and she felt it most from Fausto, even though he didn't say a word. When she dared look at him again he looked so severe and unimpressed that she felt quite overwhelmingly that she could not continue to stay there. She would not fulfil Fausto Danti's obviously low expectations of her and her family; she would not let him tease her for another instant with his mocking looks and his almost-kisses.

'Then it looks like I don't need to be here at all,' she said in a voice of patently false brightness. 'I'll call a cab to take me to Guildford—the trains will still be running from there.'

'Oh, no,' Chaz exclaimed, just as she'd feared he would. 'We can't send you away now. Stay the weekend, along with Jenna. I'm sure we could all use the company.'

'I can't...' Liza began. She knew insisting on leaving now would be rude, but she was frustratingly, furiously aware of Fausto's fulminating silence, and she wondered if he thought she and Jenna had orchestrated the whole thing, for some nefarious, mercenary purpose, no doubt. *Gold-diggers*, the pair of them. How she disliked the man, even if she *still* wished he'd kissed her.

'You can certainly stay,' Chaz insisted, and then, to Liza's humiliation, he turned to Fausto. 'Can't she, Danti?'

'Liza must do as she pleases,' Fausto replied with a

shrug. Inwardly, everything in Liza writhed with humiliation at his dismissive tone.

'Then it's settled. You'll stay.'

'I don't have any clothes or toiletries,' Liza protested, determined to make one last attempt at departure.

'That's no trouble.' Chaz airily waved away her concern. 'We've got loads of extra shampoos and things like that, and you look about the same size as my sister Kerry. In fact, I think she has a dress just like that one.' He smiled easily, as carefree as a little boy, while Liza flushed. So that was where Fausto had found the dress.

'Thank you, this is really kind of you,' she said dutifully, because she knew she could give no other response.

'I'll show you to our room,' Jenna suggested, and Chaz nodded.

'Yes, we're eating at eight—not too long now. I'll see you then?' He smiled hopefully at them both, and Liza nodded.

'Thank you,' she said again, and she turned away, making sure not to catch Fausto Danti's eye.

As soon as they were upstairs, Jenna launched into a glowing description of all Chaz had done for her. 'He's so nice, Liza, I mean really nice. You don't often meet people who are good all the way through.'

'You are,' Liza said with a smile. Her sister was so big-hearted, so generous with her time and talents, that Liza felt small for ever having resented her for a millisecond. Andrew Felton was *not* Jenna's fault.

Jenna had ushered her into a room that was twice as big as their flat, with huge windows overlooking a terraced garden, the kind you'd normally have to pay to look at.

'I mean it, though,' Jenna insisted, as if Liza had contradicted her. 'He really is a good person.'

'I believe you.' Liza reached for her sister's toiletries bag and started to tend to her frizzing hair. 'That being the case, though,' she asked mildly, 'why did you send me that text?'

Jenna had the grace to grimace guiltily. 'I'm sorry. I don't think I should have, really. It's just I was feeling so low. My head was aching and everyone besides Chaz seems so…well, I don't like to criticise, but they're…'

'Snobs?' Liza filled in succinctly and Jenna shrugged.

'I suppose, although they're all very nice on the surface, Chaz's sister Kerry in particular. She was cosying up to me right from the beginning, acting *so* sweet, but I had the feeling she'd talk behind my back the second I was out of the room.'

'She probably would,' Liza agreed.

'You've never even met her,' Jenna couldn't help but protest, and Liza sighed.

'I don't need to, but you're right, I should reserve judgement until I do.' Not that Fausto Danti ever did. Checkmating him had been one of the greatest pleasures of her life, although in truth she would rather he'd kissed her.

The thought appalled Liza as soon as it had formed in her head. No, of course she wouldn't have wanted *that*. She couldn't. She actually loathed the man, even if she was helplessly attracted to him.

And if he'd kissed her it would have been either to

toy with her or mock her, not out of genuine desire. Of that she was sure. He liked her even less than she did him, and worse, he made her feel so *small*, and she hated that most of all. She had vowed never to feel like that again, and yet here she was.

'You'll meet them all at dinner, anyway,' Jenna said. 'And then you can see for yourself.'

'Do you have anything I can wear? This dress belongs to Chaz's sister, and I really don't feel like turning up in it.'

'I only brought one dress,' Jenna said apologetically. 'And I think it's going to pale in comparison to what everyone else is wearing. They're all millionaires, Liza. They all went to the same private schools, and know the same small group of people. Some of them have such toffee-nosed accents I can barely understand them.'

'Oh, *deah*,' Liza mocked, putting on a drawling aristocratic accent as she planted one hand on her hip. '*Howevah* will we manage?'

Jenna smiled and then let out a giggle, and Liza rolled her eyes. 'Honestly, I think these people are ridiculous, looking down their noses at us just for being *normal*. They're the odd ones, really.' She gestured to the enormous bedroom with its sumptuous silk hangings and ornate furniture. 'Who really lives like this any more?' She wasn't going to be cowed by all the money. She didn't care about it. And she certainly wasn't going to let Fausto Danti think she or her sister were gold-diggers…not that she could do anything about that, unfortunately.

'They do, obviously.' Jenna narrowed her eyes as she

regarded her shrewdly. 'These people,' she repeated, 'or just one man in particular?'

Liza stilled, willing herself not to blush, but she did anyway. 'I don't like Fausto Danti,' she said frankly as she turned away to focus on her hair, and hide her flushed face from her sister. 'He's an arrogant snob.'

'A *gorgeous* arrogant snob. When we came into the study, it almost looked as if he was about to kiss you.'

'He wasn't!' Liza exclaimed, her face ever hotter. She scrunched her curls with firm, hard hands. 'We were just looking at the chessboard. I'd checkmated him.'

'That's no surprise,' Jenna answered. 'I can't remember the last time you lost a game.'

'He's annoying,' Liza declared. 'I suspect he thinks we're here as gold-diggers or something like that.'

'Gold-diggers!' Jenna sounded horrified at the prospect. 'He didn't actually say that, did he?'

Liza decided not to mention the comment she'd heard last week at the cocktail bar. She knew it would only distress her sister. 'He didn't have to.'

'Oh, Liza.' Jenna shook her head. 'Sometimes I think you're as snobby as him, only in reverse.'

'I'm not,' Liza insisted. 'I just want to take people as they truly are.' Not, she thought darkly, as someone like Fausto Danti saw them. She didn't judge the way he did, and she wasn't nearly as proud. She wasn't proud at all. In fact, quite the reverse. She knew she struggled with her self-esteem, not that she'd ever apprise Fausto of that fact.

'Well, take them as they are in an hour,' Jenna said with a sigh. 'We'll have to face everyone at dinner and even though I feel better now I'm glad you're with me. It's like going into the lion's den sometimes.'

Just as she'd felt with Fausto. Liza continued to fluff her hair as she met her sister's gaze in the mirror and smiled with determination. 'I'm glad I'm here too,' she said, and she hoped she meant it.

Fausto sipped the pre-dinner sherry one of Netherhall's staff had served as he observed the other guests circulating in the drawing room before dinner was called. Chaz was talking to Oliver, one of his rather bumbling friends from prep school, a keen cricketer who had far more money than sense. Chaz's sister Kerry was whispering with her friend Chelsea, a hotel heiress in a slippery gold sheath dress. Both of them kept shooting him coquettish looks which Fausto chose to ignore. Where were Jenna and Liza? It was three minutes past eight. They were late.

Not, Fausto told himself as he tasted the sweet sherry with a slight grimace, that he was eagerly awaiting their arrival. Of course he wasn't. The afternoon with Liza had been surprisingly pleasant, and he'd spent the intervening hours thinking far too much about her—from that electric almost-kiss that had been, in its own way, a more satisfying and passionate experience than the last time he'd actually been with a woman—to the fact that she'd trounced him in chess in just a few short minutes. She was, he admitted reluctantly, a superior sort of woman. Sadly, that still didn't make her suitable for a man in his position, with his responsibilities, his expectations. *His past.*

'Jenna!' Chaz sprang away from his friend as the

sisters came into the drawing room. Jenna was wearing a rather worn-looking black dress, the kind a hostess at a restaurant might wear, and Liza was still in the cranberry knit dress Fausto had given her, although at least she'd found a pair of flats and styled her hair into a loose knot. Compared to the other women in their designer cocktail dresses and stiletto heels, the Benton sisters looked woefully underdressed, and yet he still found he preferred Liza's unadorned simplicity to the other women's obvious attempts.

Chaz had put his arm around Jenna as he ushered her into the room, and Liza came in behind them, head held high, gaze averted from Fausto's in what he suspected was a deliberate snub, a fact which both amused and annoyed him.

'Goodness,' Kerry remarked in a clipped, carrying voice. 'You aren't wearing my dress, are you?' She let out a tinkling little laugh, like the breaking of glass.

Liza flushed and lifted her chin another inch; any further and she'd be staring at the ceiling. 'I think I probably am,' she admitted with stiff dignity. 'I'm afraid I arrived without a change of clothes, and I was caught in the rain.'

'I gave it to her, Kerry,' Fausto interjected in a deliberately bored drawl. 'I didn't think you'd mind.'

Kerry could hardly say she did mind, and so she contented herself with merely raising her eyebrows and giving Chelsea a disbelieving look. Chelsea tittered, and Liza flushed harder but to her credit said nothing. Fausto realised afresh how much he disliked Chaz's sister.

'Perhaps you should consider giving it to her,' he

remarked. 'I think it suits her colouring far more than yours.'

'I'm sure it doesn't,' Liza intervened quickly. 'But thank you, Kerry, it's very kind of you to lend your clothes to a stranger.'

'We're not strangers now,' Chaz insisted in a jolly voice. 'Since we're spending the rest of the weekend together. Now that we're all here, let's eat!'

The dinner was, as Fausto had expected, quite interminable, save for the pleasure of looking upon Liza when he could. She'd purposely seated herself as far from him as possible, which again gave him that push-pull sensation of both annoyance and amusement. Was she putting herself out of the way of temptation, or did she really dislike him that much? What he knew she didn't feel was indifference, and that knowledge satisfied in a deep and primal way.

The chatter and gossip during the meal bored him completely, however, and he stayed silent through it all, despite Kerry's obvious attempts to engage him in flirtatious conversation. He hoped his silence was discouragement enough, but he suspected with a woman like Kerry it would not be. Still, that was a problem for another day.

As for Liza…she ate her meal quietly, gaze lowered and yet alert, and he sensed she was listening to every word and finding it all as tedious as he was, a thought that gave him unexpected pleasure.

After dinner they all retired to the house's high-tech media room, where Chaz put on music and Kerry mixed cocktails. Chelsea draped herself over a leather sofa as artfully as possible, and Oliver sprawled on another as he scrolled through his phone. Jenna was chatting to Chaz, and Liza sat alone, looking serenely composed. Fausto walked over to her.

'How are you finding the company?' he asked, and she looked up at him, hazel eyes wide and clear, her mouth curving into a slight smile.

'I find them as I see them.'

'A scathing indictment, then.'

'Actually, I've found the whole evening quite entertaining. You all live in your cosy little world, don't you?'

Fausto drew back at that matter-of-fact remark. 'What is that supposed to mean, exactly?'

Liza shrugged slim shoulders. 'Only that this is quite a rarefied way of living. You don't seem to have any of the paltry concerns most people do.'

'Is that a criticism?'

'Merely an observation.'

'I suppose you're right, in a way,' Fausto said after a moment. He didn't know whether he felt glad or irritated that she'd chosen to highlight their differences. It was a needed reminder, in any case. As much as he enjoyed Liza's company, he could never consider her seriously. His family obligations as well as his own history made sure of that.

'You certainly don't seem to be enjoying the evening,' Liza told him with a laugh. 'I've been watching you scowl. Do you find everyone disagreeable, Mr Danti?'

'You should call me Fausto.'

'I've been calling you Fausto in my head,' she admitted blithely, 'but you seem like the sort of person who would want everyone to address you appropriately.'

'I don't need people to bow and scrape, if that's what you mean,' Fausto said sharply. He might have ideas about his position, and of respect and honour, but he had absolutely no need for people to be servile. The thought was repugnant to him. 'But if you really do want to get it right, it's Conte, not Mr.'

She looked startled, but then her expression cleared and she smiled and nodded. 'Of course it is,' she said, and Fausto felt frustratingly inferior for having mentioned his title. He hadn't intended to; he rarely used it. 'In future I shall address you as such. Is that Conte Danti, or the Conte of Something-or-Other?'

'Conte di Palmerno,' he bit out. 'But, as I said, there is no need. I am not accustomed to being addressed that way and, in any case, it's a courtesy title only. Officially, nobility was abolished in Italy in 1946.'

'In that case, it's Fausto all the way,' Liza quipped, and Fausto gave a tight-lipped smile. He could not help but feel she'd somehow got the better of him in the conversation.

'What I really want to know,' he said as he stepped closer to her, 'is how did you get so good at chess?'

Her eyebrows raised as her smile widened. 'You weren't expecting it.'

'You led me to believe you were a beginner.'

'I did not,' she returned. 'You assumed it.'

He paused, and then realised she was right. He h*ad* assumed it, but it had seemed like a very justifiable assumption to make. 'You're very good,' he remarked.

'Better than you,' Liza agreed, her eyes sparkling, and Fausto let out an unwilling laugh.

'Perhaps we should have a rematch.' He hadn't meant

those words to be so laden with innuendo…had he? Because now he wasn't thinking about the pieces on the board, but the kiss that had so very nearly happened over it. The kiss he wanted—*needed*—to happen again.

This rematch, he realised, was merely a pretext to get her alone, and as Liza looked up at him, eyes wide, lips slightly parted, he thought she must know it.

'Are you sure you're up for a rematch?' she asked softly, and there was no mistaking the subtext in the tremble of her voice, the way her gaze lowered and her chocolate-coloured lashes skimmed her cheeks. He ached to touch her.

'Quite sure,' he said, his low voice husky. 'Quite, quite sure.'

'What on earth are you two talking about?' Kerry called from the cocktail bar. 'You look *awfully* serious.'

'We were talking about chess,' Liza called back lightly, although her voice wavered a little. 'Fausto is insisting on a rematch after I trounced him.'

'You did not *trounce*,' Fausto felt compelled to point out.

She turned back to him with glinting eyes. 'Oh, no? You thought I'd lost my queen for no good reason.'

That much was true, and he could not deny it. He inclined his head in acknowledgement instead, and Liza laughed out loud.

'Come have a cocktail, Fausto,' Kerry said petulantly. 'I've made you a gin sling.'

'I only drink whisky and wine,' Fausto replied. 'But thank you anyway.'

'I'll drink it, if you like,' Liza offered, and with a challenging spark in her eyes she walked over to the bar, her gaze meeting Fausto's as she tossed back the cocktail. He watched her, caught between admiration, amusement and an overwhelming, heady desire. He didn't care whether she was suitable or not. He just wanted to be with her alone.

'Delicious,' Liza pronounced to Kerry, but she was still looking at Fausto. He nearly groaned aloud at the invitation in her eyes. Did she even know it was there? How did everyone in the room not see and feel what was practically pulsing between them?

'That rematch,' he said, the words bitten out. 'Now.'

'For heaven's sake, it's only chess,' Chaz interjected with a laugh.

Kerry was regarding them both with narrowed eyes. 'Why don't you bring the board in here?' she suggested all too sweetly. 'We can all play, have a tournament.'

'You don't play, Kerry,' Chaz pointed out, and Kerry shrugged impatiently.

'I know the rules, at least.'

Fausto didn't think Kerry had any interest whatsoever in playing chess, but he wasn't about to belabour the point. 'As you wish,' he said instead, and then he turned to Liza. 'Will you help me fetch the board and pieces?'

A flush rose on her cheeks as she nodded. At last they would have a few minutes alone.

With eyes only for Liza, Fausto left the room, his breath coming out in a relieved rush when she followed.

CHAPTER FIVE

THEY WALKED IN silence from the media room, down a long, plushly carpeted hall towards the study. The house yawned darkly in every direction, silent and empty. Liza wondered if Fausto could hear the thudding of her heart.

She couldn't believe how flirtatious she'd seemed, how confident. Something about Fausto's manner, his undivided attention, had made her sparkle, and she relished the feeling even as she tried to caution herself. Not to read emotions into a conversation where there weren't any, because heaven knew she'd done that before.

'Why on earth would you think I was interested in you, even for a second?'

She banished the mocking voice of memory as she focused on the present. She didn't think she'd been imagining the undercurrent of sexual innuendo in her and Fausto's conversation. At least, she hoped she wasn't. Every time Fausto looked at her, her whole body tingled. She felt as if she were electrically charged, as if sparks might fly from her fingers. If Fausto touched her, she'd burn up.

And yet he *had* to touch her. She couldn't bear it if he didn't. She might dislike the man, but she needed him in a way she had never needed anyone before—elementally, at the core of her being. And he seemed to need her in the same way, at least in this moment. And being needed, even if just for now, just for *this*, was a powerful aphrodisiac. She wouldn't let herself think about anything else.

Finally they were at the study, and Fausto pushed the door open so Liza could step first into the darkened room, her shoulder brushing his chest as she passed him. She heard him inhale sharply, and she thrilled to the sound. She felt dizzy with desire, and yet he hadn't even touched her yet.

But he would…wouldn't he? He *had* to.

She walked towards the table in front of the fire where the chessboard lay, Fausto's king still toppled from their match. Unthinkingly, she picked it up, the marble cool and smooth in her fingers. She felt Fausto standing behind her, a powerful, looming presence, and then she turned.

She could barely see him in the shadowy room, but oh, she could feel him. The chess piece fell from her fingers with a clatter as Fausto laid one hand against her cheek. His palm was warm and rough and frankly wonderful.

For a suspended moment they were both silent and still, his hand on her cheek, his gaze burning into hers. Silently asking her permission. And she gave it, leaning her face into his palm for a millisecond before his lips came down hard on hers. Finally, *finally*, he was kissing her.

And what a kiss it was. Hard and soft, demanding and pleading, taking and giving. Liza had never, ever been kissed like this. She backed up against the table, and then Fausto hoisted her right onto the chessboard, scattering the pieces as he deepened the kiss, plundering her mouth and claiming her as his own.

Her hands fisted in the snowy white folds of his dress shirt as he pressed his hard, powerful body against hers and the kiss went on and on. She tilted her head back as he began to kiss her throat, his hands sliding down her body to fasten on her hips.

Her breath came out in a shudder as his lips moved lower, to the V-neck of her dress. Everywhere his lips touched her, she burned. Her whole body felt as if it were on fire, as if she had only just finally come wonderfully, twangingly alive.

And then a voice, as petulant as always, floated down the hall. 'Fausto? Where *are* you?'

They both froze for a millisecond and then Fausto stepped quickly away, pushing his hair back from his forehead as he strove to control his breathing. Liza leapt off the chessboard, humiliatingly conscious of her dishevelled clothes, her flushed face and swollen lips, not to mention the fact that she'd been sprawled across a chessboard of all things, ripe for the taking.

'Forgive me,' Fausto said in a low voice as he stooped to gather the chess pieces, and Liza realised that wasn't at all what she'd wanted him to say in such a moment.

She began to gather some of the fallen pieces as well, and just a few seconds later the light flicked on and Kerry was standing in the doorway, her hands fisted on her hips.

'Well.' She let out a high, false laugh. 'If I didn't

know any better, I'd think something had been going on here.'

'Don't be ridiculous,' Fausto said shortly, and Liza did her utmost to school her expression into something bland. *Don't be ridiculous*?

Of course it was ridiculous, for something to have been *going on* between them. Ridiculous to him. She didn't have the space or time to be hurt by Fausto's instantaneous denial, and so she focused on gathering up the pieces while he grabbed the chessboard. No one spoke, but the air felt thick with tension.

Liza's body still tingled everywhere. Her lips both trembled and stung. She'd never been kissed like that in her life. She felt as if she'd been changed for ever, branded somehow, and the intensity of her reaction scared her.

I don't even like him, she reminded herself rather frantically, but the words seemed hollow even in the privacy of her own mind.

'So, a tournament,' Fausto said without any enthusiasm, and Kerry gave him a narrow look while Liza looked away. She wanted this evening to be over.

Unfortunately, it wasn't; the three of them trooped back to the media room where everyone was swilling cocktails. Chaz had put on a film that no one seemed to be watching, and the prospect of a chess tournament was dismissed without a word. Fausto stood in the back of the room, his hands in his pockets, while Liza went over to Jenna.

'I think I'll go upstairs,' she whispered. 'It's been a long day.'

'Oh, but…' Jenna glanced at Chaz, and Liza patted her arm.

'You stay. I don't mind an early night.' It wasn't even that early by her standards, already nearly eleven, and she felt more than ready for bed.

She said her goodnights to everyone, ignoring Fausto, who was scowling by the door; she had no choice but to walk by him on her way out. She tensed as she passed him and for a second she thought he'd speak, but he didn't, and neither did she.

Liza walked out of the room and upstairs on unsteady legs. Her whole body felt like a bowlful of jelly, wobbly and weak. As she closed her door and then collapsed onto the king-sized bed, she had an urge both to laugh wildly and burst into tears. *What had just happened?*

Well, she knew what had happened, of course. Fausto Danti had kissed her senseless. And while it would be a wonderful memory to hold onto, she was sensible enough to realise—at least she hoped she was—that it hadn't *meant* anything. Fausto disdained her as much as he ever did, and she disliked him. Mostly. Flirting a little over chess of all things certainly didn't change that.

And yet…and yet…the feel of his lips on hers, his *hands* on her…the wild passion and yet the surprising tenderness…

'Oh, come *on*,' Liza muttered to herself as she punched her pillow. 'Don't be like this again. Get a grip.'

She wasn't going to fall for the first pair of pretty eyes that made her feel special. Not like she had with Andrew, when she'd believed his flattery and made a fool of herself. She had promised herself she wouldn't fall for that again, and so she hadn't.

She knew very well that Fausto wasn't interested in her, not really, and in any case there hadn't been any simpering compliments involved, not like there had been with Andrew.

Just overwhelming mutual physical attraction…

With a groan, determined to put it all out of her head, Liza got ready for bed. She folded up Kerry's dress and took a T-shirt of Jenna's to sleep in, the excitement of the kiss draining out of her like flat champagne as she realised all the awkwardness that would likely ensue as a result. Fausto's 'Forgive me' most certainly meant he'd regretted his actions almost immediately; tomorrow he would apologise again, if he didn't just ignore her completely. Both prospects made Liza feel miserable, and she wished, quite desperately, to go home.

Eventually she fell asleep, barely stirring when Jenna came in several hours later, and then waking up a little after dawn, a feeling like lead in her stomach. She did not want to see Fausto Danti again. She had an awful feeling when she did he would be colder than ever, as disdainful and dismissive as he'd been that first night at Rico's, only this time, instead of annoying her a little, it would actually hurt.

She knew she wasn't particularly desirable or interesting; she'd already felt a bit lost in the shuffle even before Andrew had dealt her self-confidence its seeming death blow. To think, even for a moment, that she could hold the interest of a man like Fausto Danti…

Of course she couldn't. And she wouldn't let herself want to.

In any case, none of it turned out as Liza had expected. Jenna was brimming with shy excitement about her evening with Chaz, and his promise to take her out to dinner when they were back in London, and no mention was made of Fausto at all.

By the time Liza headed downstairs, dressed in an outfit of Jenna's that swam on her smaller frame, her stomach was seething with nerves and she only picked at the generous buffet that had been laid out for breakfast. She jumped every time someone spoke or came to the door; Kerry strolled in, yawning and bored, and Chelsea and Oliver were both clearly hung over, although Chaz was in as good spirits as ever.

Liza wasn't brave enough to ask where Fausto was, and it was only as they were planning their activities for the day that she learned the truth.

'It's too bad that Danti had to leave this morning,' Chaz said with unaccustomed gloominess. 'He promised me he'd stay until tonight.'

'Why did he leave in such a rush?' Kerry asked with a pout, and Liza stared down at her plate. Chaz mentioned something about him needing to work but she was afraid she knew the truth. Fausto Danti had left because he couldn't bear to see her again.

Fausto shrugged off his coat as he strode through the office of Danti Investments, located in a beautiful Georgian building overlooking Mayfair. It was empty on a Sunday morning, which suited him perfectly because he wanted to work. He wanted to work and forget a beguiling sprite named Liza Benton even existed.

It had been, Fausto had ample time to reflect on the

journey back to London, utterly foolish to have kissed her, and kissed her so thoroughly at that. In the moment he'd been inflamed by his desire and he'd completely lost any power of rational thought. It was only afterwards, when Kerry had come in looking so suspicious, and Liza had looked so dazed and overwhelmed, that he'd realised what a mistake he'd made.

The last thing he needed was gossip—or any kind of attachment, physical or otherwise. He didn't want to act dishonourably, and neither did he wish to hurt Liza, and he feared he had by sending out an entirely wrong signal. He wasn't interested in her, didn't care about her, and had no desire to make it seem as if he did.

And yet… Fausto sat back in his desk chair, his unseeing gaze on the gracious view of Mayfair out of the window; his mind's eye was occupied entirely by one woman.

Perhaps he was attributing too much tender feeling on Liza's part. Heaven knew he'd made that mistake before, with Amy.

Amy… For a second he pictured her laughing eyes, her long golden hair, the way she'd smiled and teased and made him feel so light-hearted, as if anything was possible, as if for once the weight of his world and all the responsibility he bore didn't rest so heavily on his shoulders.

Then he thought of her look of regret when she'd said goodbye to him, with his father's cheque in her hand. Yes, he knew about gold-diggers, and how guileless they could seem. Look at Jenna, with that overblown cold she'd dreamed up to take Chaz's attention. It had, to his mind, been glaringly obvious. Was Liza's response to him some of the same? Were both sisters hoping to snag rich husbands, or perhaps just rich benefactors?

Maybe all these tender feelings he feared she had for him were nothing more than a blatant ruse to keep him dangling on the hook so she could reel him in. Maybe he didn't need to worry about Liza Benton's feelings at all.

The prospect brought both a necessary relief and an unsettling irritation. He didn't like the thought that Liza was mercenary, and deep down he didn't truly believe she was. Yet the alternative was to think she might care about him, and that was just as unwelcome a thought. He never should have kissed her, even as he was thinking about doing it again.

What he should do, Fausto acknowledged irritably, was forget the whole episode completely, and yet somehow that seemed impossible. With a grimace of disgusted impatience, he pulled his laptop towards him and started to work.

Fausto managed to convince himself that he hadn't thought of Liza for an entire fortnight—almost. The energy and thought he expended in *not* bringing her to mind might have told another story, if he cared to listen to it. He did not.

He worked long hours that precluded thought about anything other than the business at hand, and he returned home to the townhouse that had been in the Danti family for over a hundred years with nothing in mind except food and sleep. And so two weeks passed well enough.

In fact, Fausto kept Liza Benton so well out of mind that when he stopped by his godfather's business one

Friday afternoon in mid-November to fulfil a promise of saying hello, he stared in complete and utter incomprehension as Liza herself looked up from her desk and stared back at him in the same way.

'What…?' Her voice was a faint thread of sound. 'What on earth are you doing here?'

She looked so achingly beautiful, and he thought he saw a spark of hope in her eyes, but the feeling of being completely wrong-footed in the moment had him retreating into chilly reserve.

'I'm here to see my godfather, Henry Burgh. I had no idea you worked here.'

Something flashed across Liza's face—Fausto thought it was hurt—and then she drew herself up. 'And I had no idea you were his godson,' she answered. 'How did that come to be?'

'Henry was my father's tutor in university,' Fausto said, his voice decidedly cool. 'They were very close. I've known him all my life.'

'I see.' She rose from behind her desk, slim and elegant in a navy pencil skirt and ivory blouse, her usually wild hair pulled up into a neat chignon, although a few wayward curls escaped to frame her lovely face. 'I'll let him know you've arrived.'

Fausto watched in frustrated silence as she crossed the room, the only sound the click of her heels on the parquet floor, and knocked on the door of Henry's office. As she opened the door he turned away, determined to act uninterested. He *was* uninterested. He hadn't thought of her once these last few weeks, after all, and it was far better that they resorted to being nothing more than acquaintances, which was in fact all they were.

He was studying the volumes on the floor-to-ceiling shelves when Liza returned. 'He's on a telephone call, but he'll see you shortly. He said to make yourself comfortable.' She gestured to one of the two leather settees facing each other, her face blank and composed.

Fausto resumed his deliberation of the shelves for a few more moments before he took a seat. 'How long have you been working here?' he asked as he sat down.

Liza had retreated behind her desk and made a great show of getting on with her work, pulling a pile of papers towards her and studying them intently. 'About two months.'

'That's not very long.'

'It's when I moved to London.'

'From Herefordshire, as I recall?'

'Yes, a small village in the middle of nowhere.' She lifted her head to look at him, her chin raised a little, a spark in her eyes that was definitely not hope. Was she angry with him? He supposed leaving so abruptly from the house party might have been construed as rude. He hadn't meant it as some sort of snub, not exactly. He'd just needed to get away. Not, of course, that he had any intention of explaining his reasons to her, or how much of a temptation she had been.

'Have you been very busy with work?' Liza asked after a moment, all frosty politeness, and Fausto gave a terse nod.

'Yes.'

'Chaz and Jenna have seen quite a bit of each other in the last few weeks. I suppose you know?'

He shrugged indifferently. 'I don't keep tabs on all my friends, and in any case I've been too busy to go out these last few weeks, but he did mention that he'd seen her.' And rhapsodised about how much he liked her, while Fausto had made no response.

'I think it might be serious,' Liza flung at him like a challenge.

He glanced at her, noting the steely glint in her eyes. 'I'm sure Chaz is well on his way to falling in love with her,' he agreed coolly. 'It's his habit, after all.'

Liza pursed her lips. 'Does he fall in love very often?'

'More than I do.'

'Ah.' She sat back, her arms folded, eyes still flashing. 'Is that a warning?'

Startled, he spared her a wary glance. He didn't trust her in this mood. 'It wasn't meant to be,' he said, although he realised as he answered that it wasn't exactly true. It had been, at least in part.

'Don't worry,' Liza assured him. 'I'm not in any danger of falling in love with you.'

Fausto stiffened in both surprise and affront. 'I was under no illusion that you were.'

'Well, that's a relief,' Liza drawled. 'Here I was, worried you'd raced away from Netherhall because you were heartbroken.'

He didn't know whether to feel amused or outraged by her absurd statement. 'Trust me, that was not the case.'

'No,' Liza said softly, and for a moment the mask dropped, her face fell, and she looked unbearably sad, which was even worse than her anger. 'I didn't think it was.'

The door to Henry's office opened and the older man emerged, his wrinkled face wreathed in smiles. 'Fausto! What a delight to see you after so long.'

Fausto rose and they shook hands while Liza watched, narrow-eyed, although she managed a smile when Henry turned towards her.

'Liza, I insist you take the rest of the afternoon off. I've made a reservation for afternoon tea for the three of us at The Dorchester.'

'What…?' There was no disguising Liza's shocked alarm. 'Oh, Henry, I don't think…'

'Nonsense,' her employer answered with a smile. 'You're on the clock for another hour anyway. I really do insist.' Henry's smile was both genial and steely and, managing a lukewarm smile, Liza murmured her assent.

Fausto knew better than to object to any of it, and in any case he could certainly suffer through an hour's conversation with Liza. Perhaps it would go some way to smoothing things over between them. If the opportunity arose, he decided, he would apologise for the kiss. That was the honourable thing to do, and then they could both put it firmly behind them—not that it was entirely necessary, since he didn't think they would ever see each other again. Still, it was the right decision, and one he felt satisfied with.

Yet as Henry locked up the office and they headed outside into the chilly dusk of a late autumn afternoon, Fausto was honest enough to acknowledge he was deceiving himself if he thought that was the only reason he'd agreed to this afternoon. The truth was, he was simply enjoying being with Liza again…far too much.

CHAPTER SIX

LIZA WALKED WITH Henry and Fausto towards The Dorchester in a daze. This was the last thing she'd expected. The very last thing! For Fausto to walk into her office…and now to be taking tea with him… She didn't know whether it was the stuff of dreams or nightmares.

Certainly he'd featured in her thoughts, both waking and sleeping, far too much these last few weeks. She'd tried not to think about him at all, but it was hopeless. A girl couldn't be kissed like that and then just forget about it. At least, Liza couldn't.

Still, she'd managed to give herself a very brisk and practical talking-to about the nature of that kiss, and how it had, of course, been only physical attraction, nothing more. Base and animalistic and easily dismissed on both sides. Or so she'd kept telling herself and she was almost convinced, until Fausto had walked through the door.

Now, sliding sideways glances at him walking down the street, she remembered how powerful his shoulders had felt under her questing hands, how hard and strong his chest was, how soft and warm his lips…

Everything about him made her buzz and come alive.

Still. Just thinking about that kiss had her tautening like a bow as yearning arrowed through her. Two weeks of disciplined thought flew right out of the window, and she feared she was setting herself up for disappointment and hurt—again.

Henry was chatting with Fausto, which made it easy for Liza to lag behind and say nothing. She'd stay for an hour, no more, and then make her excuses. After that she'd never have to see Fausto Danti again.

Why did that thought make her feel so depressed? She couldn't deny that seeing him again had lit her up inside like a firework, even though she hadn't wanted it to. She glanced at his profile—the hard, smoothly shaven jaw, the straight nose, those sculpted lips. He was like a Roman bust come to life, all aristocratic angles and sharp lines. *And just as cold.*

They arrived at the hotel and a tuxedoed waiter ushered them to a private parlour off the main dining room, already set with silver, crystal and linen for a high tea.

Liza took her seat, trying to quell the nerves fluttering in her stomach. She had a feeling the next hour was going to be unbearable.

'Fausto runs Danti Investments, out of Milan,' Henry explained to her as they all placed their napkins in their laps and the waiter brought a fresh pot of tea.

Liza glanced at Fausto, unsure how to handle the conversation. Was he going to pretend he'd never met her before? Why did that thought hurt her so much?

'Liza and I met a few weeks ago,' Fausto said smoothly, answering her silent question. 'At a house party. She trounced me in chess.'

'I thought I *didn't* trounce you,' she said before she could think better of it, and Fausto smiled faintly.

'I must give credit where it is due. But we haven't had our rematch.'

Liza stared at him in confusion, unsure if he was flirting or not. His voice was so light, his expression so bland, it was impossible to tell, although she told herself as sensibly as she could that of course he wasn't flirting. He couldn't be. She was just misreading signals—again—because she wanted to. The realisation shamed her although she did her best to rally.

'If you hadn't had to leave early, perhaps we could have,' she said after a pause, and he inclined his head in acknowledgement.

'Unfortunately, I really had no choice.'

What was *that* supposed to mean? Liza's head was spinning from the subtext, even as she wondered if she was reading too much into everything Fausto said. Discomfited, she reached for her teacup while Henry watched them both in smiling bemusement.

'It's always delightful,' he pronounced, 'when people I enjoy spending time with have already become acquainted with one another. Sandwich, Liza?'

Liza nibbled a cucumber sandwich while Henry and Fausto caught up on all their mutual friends, thankful not to have to contribute to the conversation. She'd barely had that thought when Henry turned to her with a smile.

'Have you ever been to Italy, Liza?'

'No, I'm afraid not.' She hadn't been anywhere. With four children and a large house, her childhood had been happy and full, but money had always been tight, trips abroad out of the question. 'I haven't really travelled,' she admitted with a rather defiant look at Fausto. She had a sudden contrary urge to remind him of how different they were, before he did. 'Or done much of anything. There hasn't been the money or opportunity, I'm afraid, but I've never minded. I've lived a very quiet life, really.'

'Perhaps that will change,' Henry suggested, and Liza gave him a small smile.

'Perhaps,' she allowed with another glance at Fausto's inscrutable face. 'Although I don't think so.'

The conversation moved on, thankfully, and Liza did her best to contribute as little as possible without seeming rude. Finally, after an hour, she rose from the table and made her apologies.

'This has been so lovely, Henry, but Jenna and I have plans tonight and I really should get back. Thank you.' She spared Fausto the briefest glance possible. 'It was nice to see you again.'

She barely listened to his murmured reply before she hurried out of the room, a breathy sigh of relief escaping her as soon as the door shut behind her.

When she got back to the flat, Jenna was already dressed to go out.

'Get your dancing shoes on,' she told Liza gaily. 'We're meeting Chaz at a new bar in Soho, and it has live music.'

'We are?' Liza couldn't help but sound unenthused. When Jenna had asked her to go out tonight she'd been hoping for a sisterly chat over a glass of wine at their local.

'Yes, and I really do want you to come. You've been

moping for the last two weeks, Liza. It's time to have some fun.'

'I haven't been *moping*.' At least, she thought she'd been doing a better job of hiding the fact.

'It'll be fun,' Jenna insisted, and reluctantly Liza went to change. At least she didn't think Fausto would be there. He hadn't mentioned anything that afternoon and he'd made a point of saying how little he'd seen of Chaz, and how busy he was with work. She was safe on *that* score, even if the realisation brought its own treacherous flicker of disappointment.

The bar was pulsing with music and people as Fausto pushed through the door, blinking in the neon-lit gloom of a place that was too trendy for its own good. He hadn't wanted to come, telling Chaz he needed to work, but once again his friend had insisted and after keeping his nose to the grindstone for the last few weeks Fausto had decided it might be enjoyable to relax for one evening, even if it was in a place like this.

The fact that Liza had mentioned she had plans and could very well be here tonight naturally had nothing whatsoever to do with his decision.

He forced himself not to look around for her as he made his way to the bar and ordered a double whisky. The afternoon with Henry and Liza had been, to his own annoyance, both unbearable and invigorating.

He'd done his best not to look at her, and yet even so his gaze had been drawn to her again and again, as helpless as a hapless moth to the habitual dangerous flame. With her hair pulled up, he hadn't been able to help noticing how slender and delicate her neck was. He hadn't been able to help imagining kissing the nape of it either.

He'd barely been able to conduct a conversation with his godfather with Liza seated across from him; every time he drew a breath he'd inhaled her perfume, a light floral scent that teased his senses with its subtly sweet notes.

Somehow, through it all, the conversation had got away from him. He'd intended to make some sort of apology to Liza for their kiss, but the words wouldn't come, especially with Henry present. While he'd done his best to be friendly, she'd done her best to ignore him. The hour had been endless and yet when she'd left in such a hurry he'd felt a deep sense of disappointment as well as frustration. He wanted to make things right between them, but he was uncertain as to how—or if Liza would even let him.

Perhaps tonight, if he saw her, he'd have a chance.

'Danti!' Chaz clapped him hard on the shoulder. 'Good to see you.'

'You're looking cheerful,' Fausto remarked as he leaned against the bar and took a sip of his drink. Chaz grinned.

'I am! You remember Jenna?' He ushered forth Liza's sister, who gave him a perfunctory smile.

'I do.'

'Jenna has given me the brilliant idea of having a Christmas ball at Netherhall,' Chaz declared. 'Wouldn't that be a laugh? Fancy dress, dancing, the works. We'll all pretend we're straight out of Charles Dickens or something.'

'More like Jane Austen.' Fausto glanced coolly at

Jenna, who fidgeted and avoided his gaze. So she'd suggested Chaz host a ball? Already practising at playing Lady of the Manor, it seemed. The suspicions he hadn't wanted to give voice to began to harden into certainty. He knew how women like this worked—was Liza one of them too? He didn't like to think of it, and yet he'd been duped before.

'You'll come, won't you?' Chaz asked. 'I'm inviting everyone. All of Jenna's family too.'

'All of them?' Fausto glanced again at Jenna, who flushed. She really was shamelessly inserting herself into Chaz's circle if she was asking him to invite her ridiculous mother and sister along with the rest of her relatives.

'I'll invite yours too,' Chaz declared grandly. 'What about that lovely little sister of yours, Francesca?'

'She's in Italy,' Fausto stated coolly. 'Thank you for the invitation, though.'

'She could hop over on a flight…'

'I don't think so.' The last thing he needed was seventeen-year-old Francesca having her head turned by some useless lout she met at a ball. Again.

'Well, you'll come, at least,' Chaz insisted, and Fausto gave a tight-lipped nod. He wouldn't be so rude as to refuse, although he was tempted to, especially if he had to deal with the other members of the Benton family shamelessly promoting themselves as they had when he'd first met them. Chaz clapped him on the back again before moving on with Jenna, leaving Fausto to drink his whisky in peace.

His gaze moved slowly, inexorably, over the crowded room, looking for those bright laughing eyes and that wild tumult of curly hair. He wasn't going to bother with the paltry pretence of trying to convince himself he wasn't looking for her; he was. He wanted to see her. He would apologise for the kiss, find a way to start afresh, as friends. She deserved that much. He did too. Liza Benton had caused him far too much aggravation and uncertainty. It was high time to put the whole thing to rest and prove to himself that he was master of his own mind, or at least his libido.

He did another sweep of the room, fighting an alarmingly fierce sense of disappointment, only to have his heart skip and his stomach tighten when he suddenly caught a glimpse of her in the corner of the bar, perched on a stool. Her head was tilted to one side, her hair wild and loose, and even from across the crowded space Fausto could see the sparkle in her eyes, the teasing curve of her lips. She looked as if she was *flirting*.

Instinctively, needing to know, he craned his neck to catch sight of whomever she was talking to, and then everything in him turned to incredulous ice when he saw the man in question—his smoothed-back blond hair, his easy manner, the open-necked polo shirt and expansive gestures so irritatingly familiar. *Jack Wickley*. What the hell was that bastard doing here? And why was he talking to Liza?

Fausto's fingers tightened on his tumbler and he tossed down the last of his whisky, appreciating its burn all the way to his gut. He could hardly approach Liza now. He couldn't come within ten feet of Wickley without wanting to punch the man. He turned back to the bar and ordered another double.

An endless hour passed with Liza talking to Wickley for most of it, before she left the corner she'd been perched in and came to the bar with her empty wine glass. Fausto, who had been tracking her every move, saw when she caught sight of him—her eyes widened as her gaze locked with his and her step faltered before she determinedly started forward again, her gaze skimming over him as if he wasn't there.

As she approached the bar she angled herself away from him, and incredulous indignation fired through him. Was she actually going to *ignore* him?

He leaned forward and he caught the scent of her perfume, which made him dizzy. 'I thought you'd be here tonight.' She gave a brief nod without looking at him, and resentment flared hotly. How dare she ignore him? 'Have you been enjoying yourself?' he asked, hearing the aggressive tone in his voice and wondering at it, but he *felt* too much to care.

'Yes, as a matter of fact I am.' Liza turned, and Fausto started at the obvious derision he saw in her eyes. Why was she looking at him as if she loathed him? She'd been sharp with him that afternoon, yes, but she hadn't looked at him like *that*.

She reached for the fresh glass of wine the bartender had poured for her. 'I hope you are as well,' she said in a final-sounding tone, clearly ending the conversation.

'I wanted to talk to you.' Liza raised her eyebrows, and Fausto struggled to find the right words, hardly able to believe that he—*he*—was being put at such a disadvantage. 'I wanted to apologise,' he said stiffly.

'For what, exactly?' she asked, looking distinctly unimpressed.

'For kissing you. It shouldn't have happened.'

'Noted.'

'I trust we can move beyond it.'

Her smile widened as she informed him with acid sweetness, 'I already have.'

And then, while Fausto could do nothing but gape and fume, she took her wine back to Jack Wickley, who was waiting for her with an all too smug smile.

Fausto swore under his breath. From the moment he'd laid eyes on Liza Benton he had not been himself—acting on impulse, saying and doing things he continued to regret. Acting the way he had with Amy, or even worse, which was utterly appalling. No more. For the sake of his family, for the sake of his own pride, not to mention his sanity, it was time to finally forget Liza Benton ever existed.

CHAPTER SEVEN

'LIZA, HURRY OR we'll be late.'

Liza glanced at her reflection one last time in the hotel room mirror as nerves zoomed around in her belly. Her family had taken temporary residence in a small hotel outside Hartington, for tonight was Chaz's Christmas ball.

Tonight she'd see Fausto Danti again and even though she'd come to despise the man she couldn't deny some contrary part of her was looking forward to seeing him once more—and she definitely wanted to look her best when she did.

Her unease around Fausto had deepened considerably over a month ago, when she'd met Jack Wickley at the evening out with Chaz and his friends. She'd been sitting in the corner of the bar sipping wine when he'd come in with Chaz's group and, seeing she was alone, he'd approached her.

Liza had been wary of him at first; he'd looked too slick and assured for her taste, and there was something a bit too brash about his manner. She'd learned not to trust men like that. Men like Andrew.

Yet after a few minutes of chatting she'd thawed a

bit; he had known Chaz from some party or other, and he was funny and charming and it was rather nice to talk to someone who wasn't giving her coldly disapproving looks half the time.

Then, after about twenty minutes of aimless chitchat, he'd stiffened, and Liza had followed his gaze to the sight of Fausto Danti glowering by the bar. Her heart had lurched towards her throat at the sight of him, even as an undeniable pleasure unfurled inside her like a flower.

'Do you know him?' she'd asked, and Jack had let out a humourless laugh.

'Fausto Danti? I should say so.' She'd waited for more, and he'd given it immediately. 'I grew up with him. My father was his father's office manager in Milan.' He'd paused, his lips twisting. 'We went to the same boarding school, in fact.'

'Oh.' She'd eyed him uncertainly for there could be no disguising the bitterness twisting his features. 'I only met him recently.'

He'd turned to her with an ugly sort of smile. 'And what did you think of him?'

Liza had hesitated. 'He can be a bit cold, I suppose,' she'd said, and then felt oddly disloyal for the remark.

'Cold?' Jack had sounded as if he wanted to say much more. 'Yes, I suppose you could say that.'

'Why do you sound as if you don't like him?'

Jack had thrown back the rest of his drink, and then shrugged. 'I don't. I don't want to bias you against the man, but you sound as if you already dislike him.'

'I do,' Liza had said, and then felt even worse.

'Not as much as I do,' Jack had stated grimly. 'Fausto

Danti cheated me out of my inheritance. Our fathers were great friends—mine died, and then his did, and it had always been an understanding between them that I would inherit part of the estate, and be given a senior position with Danti Investments. I staked my future on it—and Fausto refused to honour either agreement, even though he knew, as I did, that his father wanted nothing more than to see me take over at least part of the family firm.' He put his glass down with a final-sounding clink. 'He's also bad-mouthed me to everyone he knows, so I haven't been able to be hired by anyone decent, even in an introductory role.'

Liza had stared at him, horrified. 'But why?' She might have disliked the man, but she'd thought he possessed a fundamental core of honour, even if it was of his own particular brand.

Jack had shrugged. 'Because he was always jealous of the way his father preferred me. They never had a close relationship. And because he's petty and mean-spirited, but I'm sure you can find that out for yourself.' He'd smiled at her, shrugging aside all the bitter words. 'But never mind about all that. He's the last person I want to talk or even think about. Another drink?'

Liza had insisted she'd get it herself, mainly because she wanted to see Fausto up close, even if she didn't speak to him, and judge for herself what sort of man he was, after all that Jack had told her. She'd faltered when they'd locked gazes and he'd glowered at her, but then she'd continued on.

To her surprise, he'd apologised for their kiss, which had both irritated and gratified her. She supposed he thought he was being kind, but was a kiss something to apologise for, especially when they'd both so clearly enjoyed it? Or was he apologising because he regretted it so much, since she was so clearly not the sort of woman he'd ever kiss, never mind actually date or marry? He'd certainly made that obvious.

In any case, she'd chosen to end the conversation; Jack's words were still echoing in her ears and she'd realised that everything he had said had confirmed her own instinct about Fausto Danti—he was a thoroughly arrogant and unpleasant man.

'Liza? Come *on*!'

Taking a deep breath, Liza turned away from the mirror. She was worried her dress was a bit over-the-top, but her mother had taken everyone to Hereford for a shopping trip, and all her sisters had insisted she try this one on. Crimson in colour, it had a bodice of ruched satin before it fanned out in a full-length skirt that made her feel like Cinderella at the ball. But if every other woman was wearing a cocktail dress she'd feel a bit ridiculous.

As Liza joined them in the hallway she tried not to let her alarm show at her mother's dress—a perfectly nice evening gown in royal blue, except Yvonne had insisted she was still a size fourteen when she hadn't been for at least twenty years. She looked like a tube of toothpaste that had been well and truly squeezed.

Lindsay's dress was even more alarming—a long slinky skirt of silver lamé with a double slit nearly up to her crotch and a matching bikini top. She'd insisted it was the latest fashion, and that her favourite YouTuber had worn something similar, but to Liza it just looked inappropriate.

As she gazed at them both she realised she was thinking like Fausto Danti, all coldly disapproving—and of her family! Who cared if her mother's dress was too tight, or Lindsay's too sexy? They thought they looked beautiful, and so did Liza. She hated how Fausto had somehow wormed his way into her thoughts, changed the way she looked at her family, even for a moment.

'And now to the ball!' Yvonne declared grandly. She'd been so thrilled to have the invitation from Chaz that she'd talked about nothing but the ball since. When Liza had come home for Christmas she'd listened to her mother's plans for dresses, hotel rooms, and her hopes that every single one of her daughters might find true love in Netherhall's ballroom.

Jenna, at least, was almost a certainty; she and Chaz had been practically inseparable for the last month and Liza didn't think she'd ever seen her sister look so happy, elegant in her ice-blue off-the-shoulder dress. Lindsay would no doubt be on the lookout, but Liza wouldn't be surprised if Marie spent the whole evening in the corner with a book.

As for herself…? True love, she was quite sure, would be nowhere to be found.

As she followed her family outside the hotel, Liza did a double take at the sight of the white stretch Hummer her mother had ordered for the occasion, complete with champagne and Christmas carols blasting.

She knew she should get into the fun festive spirit of the thing, but once again she imagined Fausto's look of disdain and she could only cringe. Why was she letting him affect her this way, even when he wasn't here? She had to stop it.

'Oh, isn't everything beautiful!' Jenna exclaimed as they entered Netherhall a short while later. A twenty-foot Christmas tree decorated tastefully with silver and blue glass baubles stood between the double stair-cases in the house's main hall. Ropes of evergreen and branches of holly decorated every available surface, while a string quartet played Christmas carols in the ballroom and members of staff handed out crystal goblets of mulled wine. It was all incredibly elegant, and her family, Liza couldn't help but feel, stuck out like a lamentably sore thumb.

Well, who cared about that? She straightened her shoulders as she gazed around the crowded ballroom with determined defiance. She didn't care what these people thought. They were ridiculous themselves, caught up in their own privileged little world, just as she'd told Fausto back in October. They liked to look down at people who hadn't been born into the kind of society and money that they had, and the whole thing was utterly absurd. Who even cared?

She was, she decided, going to have a lovely evening dancing and chatting and having fun, and she wouldn't care what anyone else thought…especially Fausto Danti.

He knew the moment Liza entered the ballroom, even though he didn't see her. He felt her, like a frisson in the air, and he broke off his conversation with an ac-quaintance of Chaz's to look around the ballroom with an almost hungry air.

Fausto hadn't seen Liza since the night in the bar over a month ago, and while he'd been determined to banish every thought of her from his mind, he'd failed.

He'd thought about her all too often in the nearly six weeks since he'd seen her, and he was certainly thinking about her now. *Where was she?*

His gaze snagged on the sight of a young woman in the most absurd outfit he'd ever seen—a skin-tight silver two-piece ensemble that looked as if it belonged in a strip club rather than a ballroom. With a jolt, he realised it belonged to Liza's sister Lindsay. Amazingly, he'd managed to forget just how obvious and showy she really was. His gaze moved further to Liza's mother, who was looking both uncomfortable and excited in a dress that was far too tight for her. Fausto's mouth thinned. But where was Liza?

Then he saw her, standing slightly apart, holding a glass of mulled wine and looking a little wistful. Looking utterly *beautiful*. Her dress was nothing like those of her sister or mother—a princess-like confection of crimson satin, it flowed over her in a simple river of fabric. Her hair had been pulled up into an elegant chignon, but a few curls fell artfully about her shoulders; another brushed her cheek. Fausto started walking towards her without even realising he was doing so.

Liza remained where she was, looking around the ballroom, until she turned slightly and her eyes flared as she caught sight of him walking straight towards her. Fausto didn't know if he saw it or simply felt it, but a tremble went through her. Her fingers tightened on the stem of her glass. He kept walking.

The whole room seemed to fall away—the crowds, the music—as she remained steadily in his sights. Her eyes were fixed on him, seeming huge in her pale face, and yet she was so very lovely. Always so lovely.

Weeks of not seeing her had only sharpened his hunger, given focus and piquancy to the desire he'd done his best to banish. He stopped and stood before her, his gaze sweeping over her in silent admiration. She looked up at him, waiting.

'Dance?' he queried softly, and her eyes widened further, lush lashes sweeping her cheeks as she looked down for a moment to compose herself.

The animosity he'd felt from her the last time they'd met—the kiss, the apology, the unsuitability and the desire, the sparring and the wanting—all of it seemed to matter both more and less in this moment. Right now it felt amazingly simple and yet infinitely complicated—he wanted to dance with her. He wanted to take her in his arms and feel her body against his. Everything else could wait.

Finally, wordlessly, she nodded. Fausto took her half-drunk glass of mulled wine and handed it to a passing staff member. As if on cue, the string quartet struck up a sonorous tune. And as he'd been wanting to do all evening, all *month*, he took her into his arms.

Her dress seemed to enfold him as she swayed lightly against him, one slender hand resting on his shoulder, another clasped in his. They moved to the music, but only just. Fausto was conscious of nothing but her.

They moved together, unspeaking, needing no words. At least Fausto didn't need them. It was enough to hold her in his arms, press his cheek against her hair and feel her lean into him.

The song ended and another began, and still they danced. If people noticed or cared, Fausto wasn't aware. They hadn't said a word to one another, but he felt speaking might break the web they'd woven around themselves, a fragile cocoon of silent intimacy.

Desire flowed through him, but also something deeper. Something more elemental and yet more profound. He realised in this moment that he *cared* about Liza Benton—cared about her more than he had ever cared about any other woman.

The thought was utterly alarming. He couldn't care about her, not like that. Not like he had for Amy, when his honour, along with his heart, had been smashed. He couldn't give in to emotion or desire, not with so much at stake. Besides, his mother was expecting him to marry someone suitable from home, someone his family had known for decades if not centuries, someone capable and assured who could manage his estates and appear at his side without a qualm.

And yet, despite all that, or perhaps because of it, he knew he wanted simply to treasure this moment—the feel of her against him, the sight and sound of her, even the smell of her. His senses reeled.

Then the music stopped and they were forced to come to a standstill. Fausto kept his arms around her for a moment longer before he felt compelled to drop them. She stared at him uncertainly, and he realised he was scowling. He hadn't wanted the dance to end.

'May I get you a drink?'

'Since you took my last one off me,' she answered with a small smile, 'yes, you may. Thank you.'

The mulled wine had been replaced by champagne, and Fausto fetched two flutes. 'You seem in a better temper with me tonight,' he remarked as he handed Liza one, then wished he hadn't said anything.

'It's a ball, and it's almost Christmas,' she answered after a moment. 'I'm in a good temper with everyone.'

'That's a relief to hear.'

'You have been busy working this last month, I suppose?' He nodded and she continued. 'I don't actually know what you do. You're a Count, I know that much, but you have a business as well?'

'Yes, Danti Investments. It is one of the oldest banks in Italy.'

'Ah, yes, Henry said. Very noble.' She nodded, and he couldn't decide if her tone was genuine or not.

'How is Henry?' he asked. 'I haven't seen him since that afternoon at The Dorchester.'

'He's very well.'

'Good.'

They both lapsed into silence as the music struck up again; the spell that had been cast over them during the dance seemed to entirely be at an end. Fausto wished he could dispense with these meaningless pleasantries. There was so much he wanted to say, and yet all of it remained unformed, vague thoughts and feelings he could not give words to, no matter how much he wished it.

He was more than half inclined to take her by the arm and steer her out of the ballroom, back to the study, which would be quiet and dark. There he'd forget about the mere ruse of the chessboard and any possibility of a rematch—he'd take her in his arms and kiss her even more thoroughly than he had before. Kiss her, and then lead her upstairs…

'You're very quiet,' Liza remarked, and Fausto blinked at her, the fantasy he'd been constructing in his head falling to pieces.

'I have never been inclined to idle chatter.'

'Sometimes idle chatter can be pleasant,' she returned. 'Where will you spend Christmas?'

'In London.'

'By yourself?'

He shrugged. 'My family is in Italy.'

'You don't want to see them?'

'I need to sort out matters here. The London office has needed some attention since my father's passing.'

She raised her eyebrows. 'Don't you have an office manager?'

'I did, but he left a year ago. Where are you spending Christmas?' He did not want to talk about business matters with her, or even inadvertently allude to the disaster that had unfolded in the London office, thanks to his father's blind faith and old age—and one man's egotistical evil.

'I'll be in Herefordshire, with my family.'

'Ah, your family.' He couldn't keep his tone from sharpening slightly, even though he hadn't meant it to. His gaze roved around the ballroom and came to rest on Lindsay, who was holding a glass of champagne aloft as she twerked to the sounds of the string quartet.

Liza followed his gaze and blushed at the sight of her sister dancing with a suggestiveness that looked unbearably obscene from afar. Even from across the ballroom, it was clear that people standing nearby were either laughing at her or making shocked faces of disapproval.

'She's young,' she murmured, her face almost as scarlet as her dress, and pity stirred inside him.

'So were you once, but I doubt you ever behaved like that.'

'You sound so judgemental,' she flashed, and then strove to lighten her tone. 'Are you implying I'm not young any more?'

'How old are you?'

'Twenty-three.'

'And I'm thirty-six. So if anyone is to accuse anyone of being old…' He smiled, hoping to lessen any tension and also simply because he wanted her to smile back. She did, after a moment, and he was about to ask her to dance again, already imagining holding her and having the whole world fall away once more, when a carrying voice had them both stiffening.

'Liza, there you are! And oh, it's that Italian. Donato, isn't it—'

'Danti,' Fausto said as he turned to Yvonne Benton with a cool smile. 'It's Fausto Danti. So lovely to see you again.'

CHAPTER EIGHT

LIZA WATCHED HER mother eye Fausto with blatant curi-
osity—there were practically pound signs in her eyes—
and she tried not to squirm. Fausto's lips quirked, and
she couldn't tell if he was amused or annoyed by her
mother's blatant scrutiny. He arched an eyebrow in silent enquiry, inclining his head, but her mother didn't
notice.

Several glasses of mulled wine and a generous helping of hors d'oeuvres had not helped her dress situation, Liza noticed. Her mother looked as if it wouldn't
take more than one deep breath to have her popping
out, something she seriously hoped wouldn't happen.
As she glanced at Fausto she saw his brows draw together in a frown and she suspected he was thinking
the same thing—and hoping it wouldn't happen even
more than she was.

'I've seen so many interesting people here,' Yvonne
declared as she fanned her flushed face. 'So many
names. I've recognised several people from *You Too!*.'
She turned to Fausto. 'Do you ever read that magazine?'

He kept his face straight as he answered, 'I do not.'

'Well, you should. You'd recognise so many people

if you did! Lindsay told me there was some YouTuber here, but I'm not sure if I believe her. There are some people with titles—proper titles! You know, Lord or Lady This or That.' Yvonne sounded breathlessly impressed. 'Liza, did you see the Farringdons? He used to be a footballer and they have a gorgeous house up in Yorkshire. *You Too!* did a whole spread on it a few months ago—the most enormous kitchen with a beautiful family room, everything in white leather. Just amazing.'

'I must have missed that one,' Liza murmured. She wished she could find some way to steer her mother away from Fausto, or at least away from talking about all the guests as if they were celebrities to be gawked at. Had her mother's voice always been so *loud*? It seemed ridiculously so right now, and yet she felt ashamed that she cared. Still, anyone in a twenty-foot vicinity could hear them. Easily.

And, judging from the either amused or disapproving glances that were being slid their way, people were listening. And judging, just as Fausto was. Just as *she* was.

'And I must say,' Yvonne continued without a care for who was around, 'I think things are looking very promising for Jenna and Chaz. *Very* promising.'

'Mum…' The last thing Liza wanted was for her mother to start talking about wedding bells for Jenna and Chaz. She dreaded to imagine what Fausto would think about *that*. She tried to give her mother a pointed look but Yvonne just smiled.

'They've been in each other's pockets for two months now, haven't they? And don't tell a soul—' a rather ridiculous request considering how loudly she was speaking '—but I caught Jenna looking at bridal magazines the other day.'

'Mum!' Liza shook her head. She was quite sure Jenna had been doing no such thing but, even if she had, she would not want the news trumpeted about the ballroom.

'Just a peek, but still. Won't she have a lovely time doing this place up? It *is* looking a bit shabby, I have to admit. Some of the furniture is so old.'

'I believe it's called antique,' Fausto interjected politely.

'Oh, yes, antiques. They're all well and good, but everyone likes a bit of modern, don't they? So bright and clean.'

'There's nothing modern in our house, Mum,' Liza said a bit desperately. Their home was a hodgepodge of car boot sale and charity shop chic, with a few battered family heirlooms thrown in.

'Oh, yes, but if I had the choice I'd do it all up properly. Get everything modern. Of course I don't have the money Chaz has.'

'Where's Dad?' Liza blurted. Surely her father would put a stop to her mother's runaway tongue. She knew her mum meant well, and she might have had a little bit too much to drink, but the conversation, with Fausto listening to every word in that disdainful way of his, was beyond humiliating.

'He's dancing with Marie,' Yvonne said. 'He managed to get her on the dance floor, although she's got a face like a sour lemon. Why can't she have fun the way Lindsay does?'

Which made them all turn to Lindsay, who had her

hands in the air as if she was at a rave, her champagne glass tilted at an angle that caused drops to spray anyone who was standing nearby.

'Your daughter does seem to be enjoying herself,' Fausto remarked.

'Lindsay's always known how to have a good time.'

'Indeed.'

Liza could take no more. She hated that her family was embarrassing themselves, but even more she hated that she cared so much. She hated that Fausto was looking down on them, and she hated herself for minding something she'd never even considered before.

'I'm going to get some air,' she said, turning away from them both, although what her mother might say to Fausto when she got him alone Liza did not dare to think.

She slipped through the crowd of guests, barely aware of her surroundings—the gorgeous Christmas decorations, the sharp scent of evergreen, the candlelight and the elegant antiques her mother had called shabby. *Shabby.* Liza let out a huff of despairing laughter.

The entrance hall was as crowded as the ballroom and, mindful that she should hardly be snooping about the house, Liza went into the one room she was most certainly familiar with—the study.

It was dim inside, the chessboard still on the table by the now-empty grate, the room blessedly quiet. Here she could collect herself, but she couldn't, because when she looked at that blasted chessboard all she thought about was Fausto.

Fausto kissing her with thrillingly urgent passion...

Liza turned away from the board and went to the window. As she laid one hand upon the glass she realised it was actually a French window that led out onto a terrace that wrapped around the entire back of the house, and with one wrench of the handle she opened the window and stepped outside into the cold, clear evening.

Her breath came out in frosty puffs as she stood on the terrace under a sky full of stars and tilted her head to take in the slender crescent of moon.

In the distance she could hear the strains of the string quartet, the sound of chatting and laughter, but it felt thankfully far away. She wanted to be alone. Tears of shame stung her eyes, although she wasn't even sure what they were for. Lindsay's dancing? Her mother's blabbing? Or the fact that Fausto had been standing there, looking down his nose at them all, silently judging them as somehow unworthy. Judging her.

Or maybe she was crying for herself, for feeling so ashamed and disloyal. She loved her family. Yes, they could be a bit OTT, she'd always known that, but they had *fun*. She thought back to camping trips when they were little, and how her mother had washed all their underclothes and draped them over the trees and bushes, heedless of the nearby campers inspecting their rather raggedy pants.

The annual tradition of the Christmas quiz at the pub in Little Mayton—they were the loudest, most raucous team, and no one minded *there*. Yvonne always brought a big bottle of pink champagne as a thank you to Darren, the pub's landlord.

Countless family dinners or chaotic barbecues in

the garden, impromptu singalongs and games of rounders—she'd had a happy childhood in a busy home, and right now she felt ashamed of it all and she absolutely hated the feeling.

It was all Fausto's fault.

'Liza.'

His voice, a low thrum in the darkness, made her start and she wondered if she'd imagined it because she'd been thinking about him. Cursing him.

But no, she hadn't been imagining it, for as she turned around he stepped towards her from the study door, a dark figure in his tuxedo, the moonlight casting his features into silver.

'What are you doing here?'

His mouth quirked slightly. 'Talking to you.'

'How did you find me?'

'I followed you.'

She huffed impatiently, turning around so her back was to him as she stared out at the darkened garden. 'I came out here to be alone.'

'You're shivering.'

She was, because it was freezing and her arms were bare, but she simply shrugged off his words. She felt too muddled up in her head, too tangled in her heart, to offer any sort of coherent reply, never mind have an entire conversation.

Then she heard his footsteps behind her and his jacket dropped over her shoulders, enveloping her in his woodsy scent. He rested his hands on her shoulders, just as he had before, and just as before a pulse of longing raced through her, nearly made her shudder.

'You didn't need to do that,' she said quietly and he dropped his hands and stepped back.

'You were clearly freezing.'

Liza shook her head, closing her eyes against the night. Against him. 'Why are you really here, Fausto?'

It was a question he couldn't answer. *Why* had he followed her out onto the terrace? It wasn't like him at all, but since meeting Liza Benton he hadn't acted anything like his usual self—calm, reserved, *controlled*. He lost it all when it came to this woman.

'I wanted to speak to you,' he said finally.

'What about? My ridiculous mother? Or my worse sister? Or the fact that you think Jenna is some absurd gold-digger? I know you still do—I saw it in your eyes. Maybe you think I am one too.' She let out a little cry as she shrugged impatiently. 'Oh, it doesn't matter. I don't want to talk to you.'

'I have not said a word against your family.'

'You didn't need to! I saw you looking down your long aristocratic nose at them all. You think we're so beneath you.'

Fausto clenched his fists as he fought a rising frustration. He might not have known why he'd come out here, but it certainly wasn't to talk about the less salubrious members of the Benton family.

'I admit I find the behaviour of some of your family members to be…' he paused, wanting to be honest but not unduly hurtful '…questionable.' Liza let out another choked cry. 'That does not, however, reflect on my feelings for *you*.'

'Oh?' she flung at him. 'And what feelings do you have for *me*?'

The question seemed to hover in the air between them before falling to the ground, silent and unanswered—because he *couldn't* answer. He didn't have any feelings for her, at least any that he wanted to admit to, even in the privacy of his own mind.

Yes, while they were dancing he'd admitted to himself that he cared about her—against his will—but a relationship between them was still impossible and although part of him contemplated the idea of an affair with longing he knew he wouldn't lower himself or Liza to suggest such a thing. He knew she would take offence at the idea, as would he.

'Well?' she demanded, and then she let out a harsh laugh. 'Why am I not surprised that you won't—can't—answer? Because you can't bear to admit that you might like me at all, or find me interesting or attractive or anything else!'

'I—'

'From the moment you met me you've struggled against feeling anything for me, even if it's just basic physical attraction. Well, let me relieve you of that struggle, Fausto Danti. *I* don't have any feelings for you!'

She shrugged out of his jacket, flinging it towards him, and as he caught it he found himself catching her as well, taking her by the arms and drawing her towards him.

'Don't,' she said, a jagged edge of despair in her voice, and he looked down into those hazel eyes, now possessing a sheen of tears.

'Do you really not want me to?' he asked in a low voice, and with a cry of defeat she stood on her tip-toes and pressed her lips against his. The shock of the kiss was like tumbling down a hill, or missing the last step in a staircase. Everything felt jolted and off-kilter for a heart-stopping second, and then it all felt amazingly right.

His arms came around her, his jacket falling to the ground as he drew her closer to him, her breasts pressed to his chest, her body trembling and slender against him. Her mouth opened under his as he took the clumsy kiss she'd started with and made it his—their—own.

Once again the world fell away and the stars above them seemed to sparkle with an intensity no person had surely ever seen before; the universe possessed a brilliance it hadn't a moment ago, and he saw and felt it all in one simple kiss that blew his mind apart and overwhelmed his body.

And then Liza wrenched away with a gasp, one hand to her mouth as if she'd been hurt—wounded—by him.

'Don't,' she said savagely. 'Don't…don't kiss me like that when… Don't kiss me at all!'

'Liza—'

But it was too late; she was already stumbling past him, back into the house, away from him.

Fausto stood out in the cold, still air for several moments while he tried to calm his thudding heart, his whirling mind. *What had just happened?*

Well, he'd kissed Liza Benton—and she'd stopped it. She'd rejected him! Sheer incredulity had him emitting a sound that was meant to be a laugh but most certainly wasn't. Slowly, Fausto shook his head. Of course he knew he shouldn't have kissed her. Never mind that she'd kissed him first, he'd certainly taken mastery of it. And considering that he'd apologised for the last time he'd kissed her, a second round was definitely not a good idea.

But damn it, he could not get the woman out of his mind.

He needed to, though, that much was obvious. She obviously wanted him to! Shaking his head again, he walked slowly inside. The party was still in full swing as he came into the ballroom, feeling as flat as the champagne would be tomorrow morning, should any be left undrunk.

Judging by the way Lindsay Benton was swilling it, he doubted it. His mouth twisted in a grimace as he watched Lindsay still twerking away by the string quartet. The party was over as far as he was concerned.

He scanned the crowded room for Chaz, finally finding his friend at the buffet table. He started forward, determined to make his apologies.

'Danti! Where have you been?' Chaz greeted him with his usual good cheer.

'Around,' Fausto answered brusquely. 'But I'm going to bow out now.'

'What? Oh, no, old man, you can't do that. It isn't even eleven yet.'

Fausto shrugged his words aside. 'I'm tired.'

'Tell me, though,' Chaz said, slinging his arm around Fausto's shoulders. 'What do you think of Jenna? Seriously now, because you know how much I value your opinion.'

Fausto hesitated, knowing absolutely he was not in

the right frame of mind for this conversation. And yet…
Jenna's planning this ball, looking at bridal magazines,
seeming so restrained with Chaz… Lindsay's regretta-
ble behaviour… Liza's abandoned kiss…not to mention
his past with Amy, the way she'd taken that cheque, the
smile of regret she'd given him as she'd walked away…

It all felt tangled up in his mind, a pressure in his
chest. 'I have some concerns,' Fausto said shortly, and
Chaz's face fell.

'Seriously?'

'Yes, seriously. Serious concerns. About her family.
Surely you do as well.'

'I don't care about her family—'

'And concerns about her.' Fausto realised he meant
it. He'd been duped once; he wouldn't let his friend be.
'Are you sure she feels the same way about you? Because from everything I've seen of her, she seems…
unenthused.'

'Do you really think so?' Chaz looked as if he'd been
kicked, and Fausto felt a flicker of remorse. But it was
true, he reasoned; he'd seen nothing of Jenna Benton
that made him believe she was as head-over-heels about
Chaz as he obviously was about her…and too many
warning signs that indicated the opposite.

And if her sister's behaviour was anything to go by,
the Benton women blew hot and cold.

'I think,' he said carefully, 'that you need to think
long and hard before you proceed with a woman like
Jenna Benton. She might like the thrill of the chase, the
heat of the moment, and of course all the advantages
you might give her…' He paused, wanting to choose
his words with care even as part of him resisted say-

ing anything at all. 'But in the end, does she care about *you*, Chaz Bingham, and not everything that you might offer her?'

The words seemed to reverberate between them as Chaz regarded him unhappily. 'I suppose...' he answered slowly. 'I suppose I never thought about it quite like that before.'

'Then perhaps you should,' Fausto said, clapping his friend on the shoulder before he walked away, wondering if he'd just done his friend the biggest favour he could have—or orchestrated the worst betrayal.

CHAPTER NINE

CHRISTMAS WAS QUIET, and only kept from being completely miserable by the fact that it was in fact Christmas and Liza was at home with her family whom she loved. She did her best to take part in all the family traditions that she so enjoyed—stockings and carols around the piano, glasses of sherry while listening to the Queen's speech and hilarious charades. Throughout it all she felt a shadow of her usual self—and all because of Fausto Danti.

Drat the man. Drat him for being so arrogant, so cold...so *gorgeous*. Drat him for kissing her, and drat him for when he didn't kiss her. Liza's mind and heart were both in a ferment as she considered the damning things Jack Wickley had told her, and then the incredible way Fausto kissed. The two together were positively insupportable, and she returned to London just before New Year as miserable as she'd been before.

Jenna was miserable as well, although in a quiet way; Liza could tell her sister was flagging and she soon found out why.

'Chaz said he'd take me out for New Year's Eve,'

Jenna explained with a sad smile. 'But he hasn't called or texted me once since the Christmas ball.'

A quiver of trepidation went through Liza at this revelation. 'Have you been in touch with him?'

'I couldn't. I've always waited for him to contact me first.'

'Surely you can send him a text, Jenna! It's the twenty-first century, after all. We don't have to wait by the phone any more.'

'I know, but…' Jenna nibbled her lip, her big blue eyes full of unhappiness. 'If he wanted to be in touch, he would.'

'Maybe he lost your number.'

'It's programmed into his phone.'

'Still, who knows? In any case,' Liza insisted staunchly, 'you deserve an answer. You've been seeing him several times a week for two months.'

It took several days of convincing, but Jenna finally decided to send a text. Then it took several hours of deliberating to compose all six words of it.

Haven't seen you around. Everything okay?

The reply, when it came three days later, was unhappily short.

Sorry. Been busy.

'He's gone off me,' Jenna said with a sound that was far too close to a sob. She flung her phone onto the sofa and tucked her knees up to her chest. 'I knew he would.'

'I knew no such thing! He was crazy about you. He still is.'

Jenna looked at her sceptically. 'Then why wouldn't he have called me?'

Liza didn't reply as her mind raced. She could think of no reason why Chaz would have gone off Jenna. Unless...surely, surely Fausto wouldn't have interfered? He'd been disapproving enough of her family at the ball, and he certainly hadn't denied her gold-digger remark, but even so...

Had he said something? Could he have been that judgemental, that arrogant, that low?

'Give him some time,' Liza suggested feebly, and Jenna gave her a sad smile.

They spent New Year's Eve at home, eating ice cream and watching Netflix while swearing off all men for ever.

'I always wondered if there was something between you and Fausto Danti,' Jenna said as she dug out the last of her Rocky Road. 'Things always seemed a bit intense there.'

'Intense?' Liza scoffed. 'Intensely unpleasant. I never liked him, not even one bit.'

Jenna raised her eyebrows. 'I think the lady doth protest too much.'

'No, really,' Liza insisted. She could and would not mention the two scorching kisses she'd shared with him. 'I learned some things about him... Well, I already knew he was rude and arrogant—'

'I never thought he was rude,' Jenna interjected. 'Reserved, perhaps. Distant, but maybe he's just shy.'

'Shy—?' Liza repeated in disbelief.

Jenna shrugged. 'Some people are. I am. Why not Fausto Danti?'

Because he was rich and arrogant and titled and gorgeous, and people like that tended not to be *shy*.

'What else have you learned about him?' Jenna asked.

'It's not worth repeating,' Liza said after a moment. She felt a strange reluctance, even now, to relate what Jack Wickley had said to her. She was unlikely to see him—or Fausto—again, so it hardly mattered, and yet something still made her stay silent.

'Well, I say we need more ice cream,' Jenna said with a brave attempt at a smile, and she headed to the freezer.

January felt endless to Liza—a long, dull, dark month, where all she did was go to work and go home again. The dubious highlight was a visit from Lindsay in the middle of the month; she insisted on them all going out, this time to a nightclub in Islington. Liza didn't think she could have been less in the mood for such a thing, but for Lindsay's sake she went. She was hardly likely to run into Fausto Danti at a place like that, and she didn't.

By mid-February her employer began to show concern. 'You seem to have lost your sparkle,' Henry commented wryly as he signed some letters and handed them to her for mailing. 'Although admittedly it's difficult for anyone to retain good humour at such a dull time of year.'

Liza managed a rather wan smile. 'I'm all right,' she said. She *had* been dragging, but she was reluctant to admit it. Henry gave her a small encouraging smile that suggested he didn't believe her but was too polite to say so.

A few days later, however, he did say something. 'Sometimes it takes a new perspective,' he announced.

'What does?' she asked a bit warily.

'To regain one's sparkle. I'm planning to go to my cottage in Norfolk this weekend. My grand-niece is joining me with her family. Why don't you come too?'

It was the last thing Liza had expected 'Oh…'

'The weather is meant to be good, if a bit bracing, and I promise you the walks on the beach are quite restorative. It won't be fancy—whatever kitchen suppers we can throw together, and most likely fish fingers and chips for the little ones.' He pretended to shudder but he was smiling.

Liza was on the cusp of saying no out of habit more than anything else when she remembered that Jenna was going back to Hereford for the weekend to visit some school friends. Why shouldn't she get out of the city, see something different?

For a second she wondered if Fausto might be there, but Henry would surely have mentioned it if he was. Besides, he might be back in Italy by now. He probably was—a prospect that did not make her feel sorry in the least. Or so she insisted on telling herself more than once.

'All right, then,' she told Henry, injecting as much cheer into her voice as she could. 'That's very kind of you. Thank you.'

Three days later she was taking the train to King's Lynn, and then the bus to Hunstanton, where Henry's cottage was located. He'd decamped there the day before, but Liza had chosen to come on Friday afternoon, so as not to take up all of Henry's time with his family.

'It's so good to see you,' Henry said warmly when he picked her up from the station, as if he hadn't seen her yesterday at the office.

It was a short ride through the falling dusk out of Hunstanton to his 'cottage', which Liza quickly discovered wasn't a cottage at all, but an eight-bedroom manor house with a garden rolling down to a private beach. As Henry pulled into the sweeping drive he nodded to a navy blue BMW parked next to a battered estate.

'Ah, we have a visitor,' he said cheerfully, and Liza gave him a sharp look. *A visitor...?*

'You mean besides your family?' she ventured, even though that much was already obvious.

She told herself a visitor could be anyone, from a kindly neighbour to a distant relative, but her stomach was fluttering, her heart starting to pound, as if her body *knew*. Her heart knew.

Fausto Danti stepped out of the car.

He should have known Henry was up to something. Fausto kept his expression carefully bland as Henry parked the car and Liza slowly emerged from the passenger side, her face pale as she tried not to look at him.

It had been two months since he'd seen her, and he thought she looked a bit wan. No less lovely, but there was a certain weariness to her features that made him want to comfort her, surely a ridiculous notion. She as good as hated him, it seemed, no matter that she'd been the one to kiss him last—and if two months had thawed her dislike, surely this weekend would renew it.

When Henry had called to let him know he'd be at his country house this weekend, Fausto had decided to accept the obvious invitation. The last two months had been both dreary and exhausting, and he'd found himself increasingly occupied with work—and increasingly restless. He'd told himself he'd forgotten about Liza Benton, because he certainly hadn't been thinking of her, but as he looked at her now he realised just how much effort it had taken to keep her from his mind.

'Fausto,' Henry said as he came forward to shake his hand, 'I'm so glad you could make it.' Liza stiffened and Fausto knew for sure that she'd had no idea he would be here. 'Liza, you remember Fausto Danti?'

'I do,' she said coolly, and moved past him towards the house. Henry smiled easily, and Fausto wondered if the older man could not sense the tension simmering between them, or if he knew the nature of it and that was why he'd invited Fausto along.

It was, Fausto thought grimly, going to be a long weekend—and yet he could not deny that he was glad to see her again, if just for the sheer pleasure of looking at her.

An hour after they'd arrived, they were all in the drawing room with a roaring fire and glasses of sherry; Liza had met Henry's grand-niece, Alison, and her two young children, who were involved in a game of draughts. She stood by the fire, her hair wild and curly about her face, her hazel eyes pensive as she sipped her sherry.

She'd changed from her travelling clothes into a simple knit dress of moss green that skimmed her curves and reminded Fausto of how lovely she had felt in his arms. He nodded towards the chessboard that was set up in an inviting alcove.

'We could have that rematch now.'

She let out a huff of laughter that held no humour and shook her head. 'I'm afraid I'm too out of practice.'

'You beat me easily enough last time.' She looked away without replying and Fausto stepped closer to her. Alison and Henry were having an involved discussion, catching up on their various relations, and he didn't think they would be overheard.

'I didn't know you would be here,' he said in a low voice.

'Nor I you.' She slanted him a challenging look. 'Although you probably think I've orchestrated the whole thing.'

Startled, Fausto drew back. 'I do not.'

'You reserve that judgement just for my sister, then?' she replied, and then took a gulp of sherry.

'I have never judged you in that way,' Fausto said. He had wondered, but he hadn't judged.

Liza turned back to him, eyes flashing, eyebrows raised. 'Never?'

Compelled, as always, to both honour and honesty, he answered, 'A few doubts, I admit, but that is all.' And he could admit now—mostly—that they had been unfounded doubts. Liza had never pursued him the way Amy had. Quite the opposite.

'Oh, what a *relief*,' she drawled.

'You did ask.'

'And now I know.'

He paused, sorting through the tangle of his own

feelings as well as hers. 'You're angry with me for thinking you might have been after my money?'

She huffed and looked away. 'I don't like you enough to be angry with you.'

'You hardly sound indifferent.' She didn't reply. 'Is it because of that—or something else?'

'It is a whole range of things,' Liza snapped. 'But, more to the point, why do you care? You have made it clear that you're not interested in me, not really.' He was silent and she threw him a challenging look. 'You don't deny it?'

'No,' he said after a moment. 'I cannot.'

'And why is that?' Her voice trembled with the force of her feeling and she moved away from him, feigning interest in a book of photographs of the Norfolk beaches on display on a side table.

Fausto watched her, trying to school his expression into something neutral. He did not want to hurt her, but perhaps it was best if he stated his case plainly. 'I am thirty-six. I need to marry.'

She stiffened, her gaze still on the books. 'And?'

'And when I do it must be to a woman of whom my family approves, someone who is capable of managing my household, standing by my side.'

'How unbelievably quaint,' Liza said after a moment. 'How absolutely *archaic*.'

'I admit it is an old-fashioned view, but it is the one I hold. My position is demanding, and would be so for my wife.'

'And obviously I'm not even in the running.'

Again he hesitated, and then decided truth was best. 'No.'

She turned to him, a wild glint in her eyes. 'Because of my family, whom you obviously find embarrassing? Or because of me?'

Fausto stared at her in miserable discomfort, not knowing how to respond. Both—and yet neither. *Because of him*, he almost said, but he couldn't have explained that answer even to himself.

'Your silence is answer enough,' Liza said quietly, and she brushed past him as she walked out of the room.

He saw her again at dinner and, although Henry gave him a concerned look, Fausto brushed off his godfather's remarks. He was in no mood to explain the complicated dynamics between him and Liza Benton.

He determined that avoidance was the only sensible option for them both, and that proved easy enough to do—Liza had already had breakfast when Fausto came downstairs the next morning, and she was nowhere to be found when he set out on a bracing walk down the stretch of private beach belonging to Henry's property, hoping the brisk sea air would improve his mood.

It did not. As he walked along with his hands deep in his pockets, his head lowered against the wind, the confusion he'd been feeling gave way to a despondency he did not want to acknowledge.

He hated the quandary he found himself in, fighting an affection for a woman who thought he considered her not worthy of it. He didn't doubt Liza—not really—but he doubted himself. Love was a fickle emotion; he knew Amy had loved him once, and then been persuaded to change her mind. He hadn't realised she had, and he did not know if he would be able to discern Liza's feelings either. She certainly seemed one thing then another already, and who was he to know the difference? He hadn't before.

And then there was the fact that love was a dangerous emotion as well. He had been hurt before; he did not care to repeat the lamentable experience. Reminding himself that Liza really wasn't suitable felt like the sanest, safest option, even if it filled him with frustration.

And yet he could not deny, at least to himself, that he had come to care for her—her fire, her wit, the kindness and sensitivity she'd shown to everyone, even the children last night. After dinner she'd engaged them in a game of charades, and the sight of her being silly would have made him smile if he hadn't still been feeling so conflicted.

He wasn't in love with her, he decided with some relief; they didn't know each other well enough for that. But the depth of his feeling was clearly not reciprocated in the least, and that knowledge was both humiliating and hurtful.

Of course it was all for the best, since they could have no formal relationship. And yet… Fausto fumed. He did not want to end things this way. He did not want to be so unfairly disliked, and for what?

He lifted his head from his rather grim perusal of the damp sand beneath his feet to gaze out at the rippleless surface of the sea, glinting like a mirror under the wintry sun. Then he tensed as that old instinct took over; when he turned his head he saw a speck in the distance, a hunched figure on the sand that he simply knew had to be Liza.

He walked slowly towards her; her head was bent so

she did not see him coming, and the wind carried away the sound of his footsteps.

Her knees were drawn up to her chest, her arms wrapped around them, her hair whipped in a wild tangle around her face. As he came closer, Fausto realised with a jolt that she was crying—and he hated that thought.

'Liza,' he said quietly and she looked up, her eyes red, her face tear-streaked.

'Of course you would find me like this,' she said with a wobbly laugh, and then sank her chin back onto her knees.

'Why are you crying?'

'It doesn't matter. You don't care, anyway.'

'I do care,' he insisted quietly, and then he decided not to qualify that statement any further.

Liza looked up at him, pushing her hair out of her lovely tear-stained face. 'Well, if you must know,' she said in a wobbly voice that still managed to sound reckless, 'I'm crying about you.'

CHAPTER TEN

LIZA DIDN'T KNOW what had made her decide in that moment to be honest. Perhaps it was because she was so tired of feeling sad. Or maybe she was just trying not to care any more, when it had become so very hard to keep disliking Fausto, no matter how many reasons he gave her.

Either way, for the last two months she'd had to drag herself through every day, and all because of this man. Even before that she'd been out of sorts, everything a tangle of longing and outrage and uncertainty. She was tired of feeling so much, and yet she felt the recklessness of her words, their implicit challenge. She stared at him now, daring him to reply.

'About me,' he repeated in that voice of cool reserve she knew so well that gave nothing away, and she let out a half wild laugh.

'Yes, *you*. Are you outraged, Fausto? Disgusted? Or is it just par for the course that a woman would shed tears over you?'

'I would never wish any person to cry over me,' he said stiffly, and she sighed wearily and wiped her face.

'No. Of course not.'

He sat down next to her, his elbow resting on one drawn-up knee. The nearness of him brought a tingle of awareness, even in her teary state, along with a rush of longing *still*.

'Last night you acted as if you hated me,' he said after a moment, sounding cautious. 'Yet it seems unlikely you would cry for someone you hate.'

'That's just the problem. I want to hate you. I want to dismiss you from my mind, and instead I let myself be hurt. Again.' Her heart tumbled over at the blatant confession. What would he do with it? Why was she making herself so vulnerable, when she already felt so low? She didn't think she could bear his disdain now.

Fausto was silent for a moment and Liza risked a look at him, sitting so near to her. His brows were drawn together, his eyes so dark they looked nearly black. He looked so troubled and yet so handsome, and her heart ached because she knew she was halfway to falling in love with him, and the thought was terrifying.

No, she told herself rather frantically, she *couldn't* actually be anything close to in love with him. It had to be infatuation. That was all it could be, surely, considering how little they knew each other, how difficult every encounter between them had been...

'Again?' Fausto asked after a moment, and Liza shrugged.

'It was a long time ago, with someone else.' Even that was putting too much emphasis on what hadn't even been anything close to a relationship. 'Stupid of me to still be hurt, but it seems I never get these things right.'

'I have never wanted you to hate me,' Fausto said after a moment, his voice low, his head bent.

'I don't,' Liza confessed.

'And that is why you were crying? Because you *can't* hate me?' There was a lilt of humour in his voice as well as a flicker of sadness in his eyes, and both made her ache.

'It's most irritating, not to be able to do it,' she said with a desperate attempt at levity, and his lovely mobile mouth quirked in the tiniest of smiles.

'I can well imagine.'

'I have been trying so hard.'

'Indeed.' He turned his head so his face was an inch or two closer to hers, and her heart skipped a wonderful, terrifying beat. If he was toying with her now, she didn't even care. She just wanted to *feel* again—to feel that lovely, consuming desire, the wonderful certainty of *being* desired, and how together both sensations were enough to overwhelm her completely.

'And yet I keep failing,' she said, and she leaned a little towards him, both daring and pleading with him to close the small space between their mouths. Her heart was thudding now, with hard, heavy intent. 'I absolutely cannot hate you, no matter how hard I try,' she confessed in a breathless whisper.

'Perhaps you should stop trying,' Fausto murmured, leaning even closer, and then, finally, wonderfully, he kissed her.

His lips were as sweet as she remembered—as soft and hard, his kiss the most wonderful demand, the most urgent plea. Oh, she'd missed this. She'd needed it. Having it again felt as if the gates of heaven were opening. She was drowning in sunlight, overwhelmed with joy. Never mind it wouldn't last, or that he fought against

his feelings even more than she did. This—this alone—
was enough.

He deepened the kiss as her mouth opened under his
and she scrabbled at his coat to keep her balance, and
failed. They fell backward in a tangle of limbs, the sand
cold and hard beneath them, their mouths still locked.

The weight of Fausto's body on top of hers was glorious, thrilling—Liza put her arms about him and drew
him even closer. She felt as if she couldn't get enough of
him; she wanted to infuse herself with him, solder their
bodies together as if they were made of one pure metal.

He slid his hand under her coat and jumper as their
kiss went wonderfully on, and she jolted at the feel of
it on her bare skin.

Fausto immediately stilled. He broke the kiss, which
made her frantic, as he looked down at her with dark,
troubled eyes. 'Liza…?'

'It's just your hand is *cold*.' She let out a trembling
laugh; she couldn't bear it if he stopped now. She might
spontaneously combust if he did—or cry. She put her
hand on top of his own and, daringly for her, moved it
up higher on her body.

Fausto's eyes flared hotly as his hand covered her
breast. It felt intimate and terrifying and so very wonderful, and Liza knew she didn't want him to stop. She
arched her body upward to kiss him again, and with a
groan Fausto surrendered, deepening their kiss as his
hands freely roved over her body, creating fire wher-
ever they touched. There was nothing cold about either
of them now.

The wind whipped around them but Liza felt as if
they were in their intimate cocoon, their own sacred

world. In one sinuous movement Fausto shrugged out of his coat and she slipped her hands under his jumper to thrill at the hard planes of his chest.

Somehow their clothes were rucked aside, their breathing laboured and ragged as their kisses became more urgent and passionate, as if already they sensed the moment was slipping away from them and they were both desperate to hold onto it, to give it its full importance.

Liza sank her hands into his crisp, dark hair as his mouth moved lower on her body, tantalising her hidden places and making everything in her ache for more.

Her hands clenched his shoulders as she urged him on, wanting and needing even more. And he gave it— her body thrilling to every intimate touch even as the very core of her cried out for yet more still.

She reached for him, pressing one trembling hand against the arousal straining his jeans, and Fausto let out a choked laugh, his face buried in her neck.

'We should stop.'

'No.'

He raised his head. 'If we don't stop now...'

She pressed her hand against him again, letting her fingers tease, amazed at her own daring and yet knowing how much she longed for this. 'I don't want to stop.'

'*Liza...*'

'I don't want to stop. Please, Fausto.'

The moment was charged with silence, importance; Fausto lay above her, braced on his forearms, his face flushed with both desire and torment. Liza hooked her arms around his neck and did her best to draw him towards her, but his body was like a band of iron.

'Give me this, at least,' she whispered, 'if nothing else.' With a muttered oath in Italian, he surrendered to her, and she to him, as his body enfolded hers and he kissed her again. She lost herself to all of it—to his kiss, his touch, his very self.

The future fell away along with the past; she wanted nothing but this moment in all of its glory—even with the wet sand, the icy wind, the roaring waves. She was overwhelmed by it all, but most of all by him, his arms wrapped around her, his mouth on hers, his hard body pressed along her whole length and yet still, *still* not close enough.

She tried to unbutton his jeans and her fingers fumbled on the snap. Fausto wrapped his hand around hers.

'You are sure about this…?'

'Yes, I am sure,' she cried, half wild, and finally, thankfully, he unbuttoned his jeans himself. Then he reached for hers, and she wriggled out of them as best she could, barely conscious of the damp sand beneath her, the awkwardness and incongruity of the moment right here on the beach—none of it mattered.

'*Liza*…' Fausto said, his voice a groan, her name a plea.

She pulled him towards her. For a second he hesitated again, poised above her, their worlds and selves about to collide in the most intimate and sacred way possible.

Then Liza arched up and with a low, guttural moan of both surrender and satisfaction Fausto sank inside her.

He'd tried to resist. He wanted no regrets for either of them, but Liza—her body, her *self*—proved impossible to resist. Fausto buried his face in the sweet curve of her neck as he waited for her to adjust to the feel and weight of him.

He knew from that first incredible moment that she had to be a virgin, but he couldn't think further than that as the siren song of pleasure drove everything else out.

'Are you all right?' he managed after a moment, his voice strangled, and she let out a breathless laugh.

'For heaven's sake, yes—*yes*.'

Then, amazingly, he was laughing too, amazed to share such joy in this moment, until laughter was replaced by something far, far sweeter as he found a rhythm and Liza matched it, clumsily at first but then with greater assurance and fluidity, until they were both moving as one. They *were* one.

Fausto had never felt so attuned, so fulfilled and unified and utterly complete. It was beyond the physical, even beyond the emotional; to say it was sacred would have felt, out of the moment, absurd, and yet it was. It *was*.

Higher and higher they moved and strove, each stroke unified and glorious, until their oneness was made even more complete as their bodies crashed together in the final cymbal note of pleasure, before Fausto rolled over onto his back, breathing heavily, taking Liza with him.

His vision cleared and his heart began to beat more slowly as he became aware, in increments, of the cold, damp sand beneath him and something sharp poking into his back. Liza's hair was spread across his face, tickling his nose, and he felt her heart thudding against his like a bird trapped in a cage.

His jeans were rucked, rather ridiculously, about his

knees, as were hers. He had a terrible suspicion that if they were to be observed from afar they would look not only absurd, but obscene. The sand really did feel very cold.

He didn't know which of them moved first, if Liza stirred or if he tensed, but as one—and yet now utterly *not* as one—they separated. Liza sat up, wriggling back into her jeans, her head bent, her hair falling forward so Fausto could not see her face.

Fausto did the same, straightening his jumper and buttoning his jeans. Neither of them spoke, and the longer the silence stretched between them the worse it felt.

Fausto tried to examine his own mind, but his feelings were so jumbled—a vague self-loathing mixed with a soul-deep satisfaction—that he did not think he could utter a single coherent syllable.

Never, not once in his life, had he lost control the way he had with Liza Benton. Not even with Amy, not with *anyone*. He'd tried, heaven knew, to keep his head—and his body—but he hadn't. In the moment he'd been more than happy to sweep aside every concern, every second for pause, every perfectly good reason not to rut like a sheep on a beach in winter where anyone could happen by!

At least it was a private beach, but *still*. What if Alison's children had run up to them? Or even Henry? Fausto could not bear to think of such horrifying possibilities, and yet he had to now, as he hadn't then.

And that, he acknowledged grimly, was just considering the *appearance* of the whole thing. What about his motive, his *honour*? Liza was—*had been*—a virgin, something he thought he could have surmised before this morning, and yet he'd felt no compunction at taking her virginity on a cold, hard beach, with little romance and even less tenderness. His stomach roiled with disgust at himself and his actions. This was not who he was. This was not who his father had taught him to be.

He glanced at Liza, who was running her fingers through her hair, trying to untangle the knots. Her expression seemed composed, and yet he still sensed a fragility about her, a vulnerability that made him long to reach out and take her in his arms—yet he knew where that would go, and he had no desire to go there again.

Although the truth, Fausto reflected, was that he *did*, far too much, and that was why he stayed where he sat.

'I'm sorry,' he said at last. She let out a huff of sound that he suspected was meant to be a laugh but wasn't.

'That's about as bad as "Forgive me".'

It took him only a few seconds to remember that was what he'd said the first time they'd kissed. 'I should have acted with more restraint,' he said. 'For that I am sorry.'

She turned to look at him, her hair still in tangles about her face, her lips swollen from his kisses. 'Do you regret it?' she asked baldly, and he heard a challenge in the question. He didn't know what answer she wanted him to give, but in any case he knew he could only give an honest reply.

'Yes—I never would have chosen this.' She looked away. 'And I can't imagine you would have either—especially for your first time.' He paused, half hoping she would deny it, but she didn't. 'It was your first time?'

'Yes.' Her voice was wooden, her face still turned away from him.

'Then I truly am sorry.'

'Is that the only reason you're sorry?' she asked after a moment, her fingers plucking at a frayed thread on her jumper. 'Because it wasn't candlelight and roses and a king-sized bed?'

A more pointed and dangerous question. Fausto sighed. 'No, it's not.'

'I didn't think so.'

'Liza—please believe me, I've never wanted to hurt you.'

'You haven't,' she shot back, her voice brittle. 'Please, Fausto, don't feel guilty on my account. I was a full participant in this.' She gestured to the expanse of sand between them. 'You don't need to have any regrets.'

And yet he did. In that moment he felt swamped by them—by his own lack of self-control, by the desire that still coursed through him. By the sure and certain knowledge that he'd hurt a woman he admired and respected, and yet still knew he could never marry.

Yet why couldn't he?

The question, so unexpected, suddenly seemed obvious. Why shouldn't he marry Liza Benton? Admittedly, she would not be his family's first choice, by any stretch. His mother would be disappointed and hurt. His father would never have countenanced such a choice.

And, he acknowledged, she would struggle to fit into his world, both here and even more so in Italy. She was not from one of Lombardy's ancient families, not by any means. Not even close.

And yet…he wanted her. He cared about her. He didn't love her, not yet, and that could only be a plus. She wouldn't be able to hurt him. And, of course, she was lovely and gracious and kind.

And, he realised hollowly, she could at this moment be carrying his child. He hadn't used protection. Amazingly, he hadn't even *thought* about protection. And he had a feeling it was far too much to hope for that she might already be on the pill.

'We should get back,' Liza said in that same toneless voice that hinted at despair. She struggled to get up from the sand, and Fausto reached out a hand to help her rise. She jerked away from him.

'Liza, please.'

'I'm… I'm sorry.' She drew a hitched breath. 'I can't. I'm trying to be sanguine and sophisticated about this, but I'm finding it hard.' Another hitched breath, this one more revealing. 'I know that's not what you want to hear.'

'This isn't about what I want to hear,' Fausto insisted. 'We need to talk about this. Properly.'

'We already have, at least as much as I want to.' She buttoned up her coat with trembling fingers. Fausto rose easily from the ground as he gazed at her frustration. Only moments ago she'd been eminently touchable; now she seemed entirely unreachable.

'We haven't,' he declared firmly. 'Not in the least. There's the matter of birth control, for a start—'

She let out a ragged laugh that was lost to the wind. 'Of course that's what you'd be concerned about. Heavens, a baby born on the wrong side of the blanket! Common enough these days, but it's the stuff of your nightmares, I'm sure.'

Irritation warred with sympathy; he could see how much she was hurting and yet he couldn't comfort her. She wouldn't let him. 'That's not what I meant—'

'Then what did you mean?' She flung up a hand. 'No, don't tell me. I don't want to know. Every time you've told me what you've been thinking it's been the worse for me, and I really don't think I can handle what you're thinking right now.'

'Liza—'

'No, Fausto, please. Let's leave it at this.' She forced herself to look at him, her face heartbreakingly lovely, her expression one of both courage and fragility. 'You don't need to feel any regrets. I won't. What happened here was—well, it was amazing.' She let out a trembling laugh. 'The most amazing experience of my life, so thank you, actually.' Another laugh, this one full of tears. 'And that's…that's all I'm going to say about it.' She started walking, hurrying past him, her head tucked low. Fausto tried to catch her arm but she shrugged away from him.

'Liza!' he called, but she shook her head and started running. Fausto knew he could have caught up with her easily enough, but that hardly seemed to be a wise course of action. And so, even though everything in him resisted, he simply stood there and watched her go.

CHAPTER ELEVEN

She had spent the last four hours hiding in her room and Liza knew her unsociability was bordering on rude. Thankfully, she hadn't seen anyone when she'd come back to the house; she didn't think she'd have been able to give an answer if she had.

She'd hotfooted it to her room and stripped off her rumpled clothing, trying not to burst into tears. She wasn't even sure why she felt like crying; she'd meant what she'd said when she'd told Fausto it had been the most amazing experience of her life. Perhaps that was the cause for her tears. It certainly wasn't going to happen again, and it had left her in a state of both wonder and longing.

She'd hoped half an hour standing under a near-scalding spray would have helped balance her mood but she'd felt even more despondent when she'd emerged, as pink as a boiled crab. She'd wrapped herself in the dressing gown that had been provided on the back of the bathroom door and curled up in bed while a bittersweet montage of moments played relentlessly through her head.

She knew she was tormenting herself by reliving

those sweet, sweet moments with Fausto—as well as the unbearably awkward and painful moments after. She'd so wanted to be sophisticated and unruffled, as if she had sandy trysts all the time, but she hadn't been. She hadn't been at *all*. She'd been gauche and prickly and so very hurt. And now Fausto Danti had yet another reason to regret her very being.

The thought of having to see him for the rest of the weekend was unbearable. To stumble through pleasantries as if they were merely acquaintances—she couldn't do it. She wouldn't. And yet to run away the first chance she got would be rude to Henry, and too revealing to Fausto. She wanted to show him she didn't care, even if she very much did.

Even if there had been a large, sorry part of her that had been hoping—waiting, even—for him to take her in his arms afterwards and kiss her tenderly and tell her he'd fallen in love with her. As if…! When would she learn? When would she remember that no man had ever remotely wanted to do such a thing?

Fausto had looked horrified afterwards. He'd acted as if he regretted absolutely everything about their encounter. He'd even said as much. And meanwhile she'd felt as if the universe had unveiled its secrets, as if the very atoms of her being had shifted and reformed. She was absurd, the very parody of a naïve, stupid virgin with stars in her eyes and hope in her heart.

With a groan Liza pressed her face into the pillow, wanting only to will it all away—even though she never actually would want such a thing. She wanted to hold onto all the memories even as she despised them. Oh, why did Fausto Danti provoke such a maelstrom of contradictory emotions within her? The sooner this weekend ended, the better.

And yet then she'd most likely never see him again…

Liza groaned again.

Eventually, knowing she needed to show herself, she rose from the bed, aching and weary, and dressed. She took pains with her appearance—fluffing her curls and applying understated make-up, even though she hated the thought of Fausto knowing she'd gone to such pains. Still, at a time like this make-up felt like armour.

Downstairs, the house was strangely quiet; when she ventured into the drawing room, Henry put down his newspaper to give her a charming smile.

'How lovely to see you! Did you enjoy the beach? The wind does take it out of one, I find.'

'It was lovely,' Liza murmured, unable to look him in the eye. She glanced around the empty room. 'Where is everyone?'

'Alison has taken the young ones into Hunstanton. Fausto was taking some business calls—but I'm sure he'll be here shortly. Perhaps he'll give you that game of chess?'

Henry raised his eyebrows while Liza blushed and mumbled something mostly unintelligible. A few moments later Fausto appeared, checking his step as he caught sight of Liza before he assumed that oh, so bland expression and came into the room.

'Fausto, I was just saying you and Liza should have that rematch.' He gestured to the board while Liza fidgeted. She had never hated chess so much in her life.

'If she wants a game, I'd be happy to play,' Fausto replied after a beat. He had showered since their beach interlude; his hair was dark and damp, brushed away from his freshly shaven face, and Liza was drawn to the clean, strong lines of him, remembering exactly how he'd felt against her. She *had* to stop thinking like that.

'It's not necessary,' Liza said.

Fausto turned to her. 'You never told me how you came to be so good at chess.'

'My father is a grandmaster,' she said, unable to look him in the eye. She moved her gaze rather wildly around the room, finally letting it rest on the chessboard. 'We played all through my childhood. I competed in junior tournaments when I was young.'

'I had no idea,' Fausto said, and she threw him a challenging look.

'Why would you?'

He acknowledged her point with an inclination of his head. 'Shall we play?'

She swallowed. The last thing she wanted to do was play a game of chess with Fausto Danti. Considering their history, it felt far too intimate—every word, every move loaded with both innuendo and memory.

'Yes, why don't you?' Henry said. Liza looked Fausto full in the face and, to her shock, his returning smile was full of sympathy. There was no mockery there, no icy hauteur, just kindness, and that nearly undid her.

'All right,' she said, her voice little more than a whisper. 'Let's play.'

Her fingers trembled as she picked up her knight to make the opening move. She could feel Fausto across the table from her—his presence, his power, the overwhelming *force* of him. It was like an undertow, pulling her down, drowning her. She could barely form a coherent thought, much less plan strategic chess moves.

They played in silence for a few minutes, the tension ratcheting up with every move, and any neat tricks Liza had been planning were just as neatly avoided by Fausto. Halfway through the game, both of them down several pieces, the game suddenly turned into something bigger, something far more important. Winning felt crucial. To lose was not to be contemplated. Defeat would be an emotional disaster, and one she didn't think she would ever recover from.

Slowly but surely, Liza felt the tide turning in Fausto's favour and she knew the game was slipping out of her control. Then, in a foolish error, she lost her queen and she bit her lip hard enough to taste blood.

'Draw?' Fausto suggested softly, and she shook her head.

'Let's play to the end.'

He won in just a few short moves, and somehow Liza managed a stiff nod. 'Well done. Good game.' She rose unsteadily from the table, feeling as if she could break. It was only a stupid game, she reminded herself fiercely, and yet it felt like just another reminder that she wasn't good enough for Fausto Danti in any way. That she never would be.

'It was a very good game,' Fausto said, rising from his chair as Liza moved blindly past him.

'I think I'll get some air,' she managed, and walked quickly from the room. She weaved through the house, finally ducking into a small morning room decorated in soothing blues and greys, although little did they help her mood. She let out a shuddering breath, willing the tears back. It was so ridiculous to cry over a chess game, and yet she knew it was more than that. So much more.

'Liza.'

Fausto's voice had her groaning aloud. 'Can you *never* let me have a moment's peace?' she demanded raggedly.

'Not when there is unfinished business between us, no.'

She took a deep breath and turned around, willing herself to have enough strength for one more conversation. 'What is it, then?'

Fausto regarded her quietly for a moment and then he closed the door behind him. 'I want to ask you something,' he said.

Liza shrugged, spreading her hands helplessly. 'What? What could you possibly want to ask me?'

'I want,' Fausto said, his voice low and firm with purpose, 'to ask you to marry me.'

As soon as he said the words, Fausto realised how much he meant them—and how shocking they sounded. He'd been thinking of proposing to Liza since their interlude on the beach, but it hadn't crystallised into both fact and desire until now. Until he'd said it out loud.

Liza's mouth dropped open and she gaped at him soundlessly for a few seconds before she shook her head. 'I was so not expecting you to say that.'

'I've said it, and I mean it.'

'Why?'

Her incredulity was understandable, and so Fausto sought to explain as clearly and concisely as he could. 'First, because I care about you. Second, because we have an undeniable physical chemistry. And third, because you could be carrying my child.'

Liza pressed her lips together, her eyes flashing. 'Why do I think it's the last one that has forced your hand?'

He inclined his head. 'Perhaps it has, but I mean it no less.'

She let out a huff of disparaging sound. 'Why not just wait a couple of weeks, Fausto? Make sure I am pregnant, because I'm probably not.'

'You have no way of knowing and, in any case, possible pregnancy aside, I still wish to marry you.'

Liza shook her head again. She still looked winded and dazed by his offer. 'You cannot possibly want to marry me.'

'It is true, I have fought against it,' Fausto said steadily. 'Considering the differences in our life situations, and the expectations my own family has for my bride, I didn't want to feel anything for you, and I did my best to avoid you.'

'Oh, you did, did you?' Liza stated with a broken laugh.

'There are obvious disadvantages to our union,' Fausto continued. He would not shirk away from mentioning the unfortunate and the obvious.

'Oh?' Liza's body tensed and her eyes flashed again. 'And what are those, exactly?'

Fausto exhaled impatiently. 'Surely they're apparent.'

'I'd still like you to say them,' she snapped, looking angrier by the second, but Fausto was no longer in any mood to appease her.

'I am the Conte di Palmerno,' he said, only to have her interject,

'I thought it was a courtesy title only.'

'Perhaps you are not aware of my position,' Fausto said after a moment, willing to give her the benefit of the doubt. 'And what it would mean to be my Contessa. The duties and responsibilities—'

'Oh, I'm sure it would be a great privilege,' Liza drawled, sounding as if it would be anything but. 'But since I didn't ask to be your Contessa, and have no desire to be your Contessa, this whole conversation is pointless!'

Fausto stared at her for a moment, shocked by her outrage as well as her defiance. He realised he had expected neither. Surprise, yes, a certain amount of caution. But to act insulted? When he was offering such a compliment and yes, indeed, a privilege? It could not be denied. 'You…you are refusing me?' he asked slowly.

She let out a hard, ugly sort of laugh. 'Is that so very hard to believe?'

'As it happens, yes.'

She let out another laugh, the sound just as unforgiving. 'Your arrogance knows no bounds.'

'I don't believe it is arrogant to be aware of all I can offer you, especially considering your own situation, and the disadvantage your family might bring—'

'*My* family!' Liza practically shouted. 'A disadvantage to you? Just because they're normal?'

'Liza, you know as well as I do—'

'And if I cared about money, perhaps—' she cut across him furiously '—perhaps I would want you to list all those obvious advantages. But, as it happens, I don't. When I marry it will be for love—because some-one loves me. *Me*, and no one else, no matter where I come from or what my family is like, or whether I'll make a good *Contessa*.'

'I told you I care for you—' Fausto protested.

'Against your will! You have fought against feeling anything for me. If I were to agree to marry you, I'd be as good as dragging you to the altar with a gun to your head!'

Her theatrics annoyed him, although he strove to stay calm. 'I assure you, I would go there of my own free will.'

'Stop, Fausto, these sweet nothings are really too much,' Liza retorted sarcastically, her tone like acid. 'The answer is, and always will be, no. Absolutely, un-equivocally no.'

He could hardly believe she was saying such a thing—and he was hearing it. In all his deliberations about whether to propose, he'd never once considered that Liza would refuse him. Perhaps that *had* been ar-rogance, but even now he considered it justified.

'May I know why?' he asked coldly.

For a second Liza looked as if she might burst into tears—her lips trembled and she blinked rapidly, draw-ing a shuddering breath before she stated staunchly, 'Because you are not the kind of man I wish to marry.'

'And why is that?'

'Do you find it so hard to believe? Do you think so highly of yourself that you can't imagine a woman re-fusing you?'

'I would not put it in such terms, of course—'

'Well, think again,' Liza cried, her voice trembling

on a high, wild note. 'Everything you have ever said or done has shown me that you are a snobbish, arrogant, rude and unlikeable person, and I have absolutely no desire to spend another minute with you, never mind the rest of my life!'

Fausto stared at her, anger warring with a deep, terrible hurt. He had known Liza was fighting her feelings, just as he was, but to impugn him so thoroughly…

'In every instance I have tried to act honourably,' he said in a low voice, a thrum of fury vibrating through it.

'Then your sense of honour is very different from mine, as well as most people's.'

Anger—and that damnable hurt—pulsed through him. He'd been called old-fashioned, standoffish and, yes, proud, mostly by people who didn't know him very well. At home, with people he knew and loved, he could be comfortable and relaxed, but a need to be formal and set apart had been ingrained into him since he was child. He was a Danti. He had to be an example. And yet Liza seemed to think he was an example of everything bad, and nothing good.

'I did not realise you held me in such low esteem,' he said after a moment. For a second Liza looked again as if she were about to cry. 'Is there something in particular that has caused you to think of me with so little regard?' he asked, and she drew a hiccuppy breath.

'Jack Wickley, for one.'

'Jack *Wickley*?' He stared at her in disbelief, hardly able to credit that she'd believed that amoral chancer over him. 'You are accusing me—judging me—based on the word of Wickley?'

She tilted her chin up, her eyes flashing fire. 'Why shouldn't I?'

Fausto could not bring himself to reply. The idea that Liza would believe every word that slimy worm had said—that, after knowing him, Fausto, more than a little, she would still judge him so unfairly and harshly...

'Well?' Liza demanded, and Fausto simply shook his head. He would not stoop to defend himself against Wickley. He could not lower himself so.

'You deny what you did?' she challenged, and he stared at her coldly.

'What is there to deny?'

'That you deprived him of his inheritance and the job your own father promised him, and spread rumours about him that he wasn't trustworthy, so no one would hire him.'

He pressed his lips together as a white-hot rage threatened to consume him. 'That is what he told you?'

'Yes.'

'And you believed him?'

'Why would I have any reason to doubt him?' Liza flung at him. 'In any case, it's not just that. What about Jenna and Chaz?'

'What about them?' Fausto asked, his voice toneless, the words clipped. Fury beat through his blood but he held it in check.

'Did you warn Chaz off Jenna? I didn't want to believe it, but I know how you were looking at us all at that Christmas ball, and he dropped her like a hot potato right after.'

'I told him to proceed carefully,' Fausto conceded

after a brief, heightened pause. 'And that I questioned her feelings for him, as well as her intentions.'

Liza's face flushed as she glared at him, her hands clenched into fists at her sides. 'You had no right!'

'He asked my opinion, and I gave it,' Fausto stated. 'He is a grown man, and he acted accordingly. I exerted no pressure, if that is what you're implying.'

'Your opinion is pressure enough!'

'That is hardly my fault.'

She glared at him for a full thirty seconds, her face full of hurt and anger, her eyes flashing fire and yet possessing a sheen of tears. 'I loathe you,' she choked. '*Loathe* you. And nothing would ever induce me to accept your horrible, half-hearted proposal.'

'Never fear,' Fausto returned in the iciest tones he'd ever used. 'Nothing would ever induce me to repeat it.' Not trusting himself to say any more, he inclined his head and then left the room as quickly as he could.

Unable to face Henry or his family, he went up to his bedroom and started to pack. He would not stay another moment under the same roof as Liza Benton. He could not believe she had treated his proposal—made in good faith and with honour—with such scorn and derision. And all because of a single word to his good friend— and Jack Wickley's damning recounting.

Fausto swore under his breath as he considered that wretch of a man. He had not wanted to stoop to justify himself to Liza, but he was sorely tempted. She thought him so proud? So snobbish and arrogant and rude and *unlikeable*? Perhaps he would show her otherwise.

Before he could think better of it, he stormed back downstairs, barely conscious of Henry peering out from the drawing room, and flung open the door to the little sitting room where he'd found Liza before.

She was still there, collapsed into a chair, her head cradled in her arms. She lifted her tear-stained face, her expression incredulous, as the door banged against the wall and he came into the room, fists clenched, chest heaving.

'You called me proud—well, I am not so proud as all that. I resisted telling you the truth about Jack Wickley because I had hoped that it would be enough for you to know the kind of man I was, rather than a stranger you met once in a bar.' Belatedly registering her tears, he realised she must have been crying, but he had no time to wonder at it as he continued steadily, 'Jack Wickley was the son of my father's office manager in Milan— a good man, who died when Jack was only sixteen. My father took him under his wing, brought him into our house and paid for his education through university, promising him a position with the company after he graduated.'

Liza, looking dazed, nodded slowly and, as the old hurt and bitterness coursed through him, Fausto made himself continue. 'I have known Jack since I was a child myself, and I have never liked him. Not because I am proud, but because he seemed crafty and sly. He cheated on his exams in school, and I discovered during university he was a terrible playboy and womanizer. Despite all that, I honoured my father's word and will, and I gave Jack the position of office manager here in London, over three years ago now. My father was ill, and unable to run the company, and I was consumed with family matters. However, upon my father's death, it became clear to me over time that Jack Wickley had terrorized the office staff, made unwanted advances to female employees and embezzled from the company to the tune of several hundred thousand pounds.'

Liza's eyes widened and a soft gasp escaped her, which was gratifying enough but, now that he had started, Fausto knew he had to continue. 'Moreover,' he said, 'I discovered that he had attempted to seduce my sister Francesca at a family party two years ago, when she was only fifteen. So if I dislike and distrust the man, surely you can understand why. I had no idea he was spreading the story you told me, so I can add deceit to his ever-growing list of sins.' He drew a breath and let it out, half relieved he'd told her everything, and half ashamed that he'd had to. 'If you doubt my story you can talk to Henry, who knows most of it, except about my sister, or Chaz. Or, for that matter, anyone in the London office of Danti Investments. The whole reason I have been here these last months is to repair the damage Jack Wickley wrought upon my company and my family.' He stared at her, his fury still pulsing through him. 'As for the matter of Jenna and Chaz, it is true I have had reservations about your sister. Perhaps they were unwarranted, but I have been fooled by a woman before.' He paused before making himself continue. 'I thought I loved her, and I brought her home to meet my family. Her true colours soon became all too clear.' And that was all he would say about that. 'I advised Chaz to be cautious, no more, and I still believe I was justified. If I was not, and your sister truly has feelings for Chaz, then I am sorry.' He let out a low breath before giving a terse nod of farewell. 'And now I will say goodbye.'

Without waiting for her reply, not trusting himself to say or do something he knew he would later regret, Fausto left the room. He made his apologies to Henry, finished his packing and had left the house before Liza had even stirred from her chair.

CHAPTER TWELVE

LIZA SPENT THE next two months in a daze. Days passed, grey and alike, and she was barely aware of their coming or going. She worked, ate, slept, and thankfully neither Henry nor Jenna nor anyone else pressed her on any point, or asked her why she seemed so very miserable.

Perhaps, she reflected, she was doing a better job than she thought at seeming normal, even happy. She went out at the weekends with Jenna; she went home to Hereford twice, and had Lindsay come to stay. She even accompanied Lindsay and Jenna to a nightclub, but she didn't dance and she left when she glimpsed Jack Wickley, of all people, come through the door. That was one person she could not bear to talk to, or even to see.

And of course there was another person she couldn't bear even to think about—although for entirely different reasons. Ever since Fausto had proposed, and then explained so much to her, Liza's emotions had been in an utter tangle. Her mind went round and round in circles as she tried to make sense of what Jack Wickley had told her, to what Fausto had told her, to what she had seen—and felt—herself. The result was a very uncomfortable ferment of uncertainty, followed by a far worse sweeping sense of desolation.

What if she'd been wrong? What if, to guard her own heart and for the sake of her own pride, she'd turned Fausto Danti into someone he never had been—someone like Andrew Felton, whom she couldn't trust and had come to dislike? Yet Fausto was no Felton, and she should have been smart and sensitive enough to see that. Yes, he was proud, but he was also honourable.

Wasn't he?

In any case, Liza reminded herself more than once, it was all too late now. As Fausto had said himself, he was never going to repeat his proposal. Not that she would accept it, anyway. She might have been wrong in her assumptions about who he was as a man, but that didn't mean she wanted to *marry* him. Even if he was an honourable man, he still had old-fashioned notions of suitability and position, and he'd made it clear he was expected to marry some Italian socialite or other, from a family he'd known for about a million years. She was not remotely in the running, for so many reasons.

Besides, the possibility of her being pregnant had evaporated within a week; there was nothing, absolutely nothing, to draw them together again.

And that prospect was not something, she told herself again and again, to feel downcast about, never mind heartbroken. Her heart was not broken at *all*.

Jenna and Henry might have acted as if they didn't notice her doldrums, but someone unexpected did. At the end of April, more than two months after that weekend in Norfolk, Yvonne called her with a proposition.

'I know you must have some holiday to take, and

your nan has got it in her head to go travelling. You know as well as I do that she can't go alone, so I said you'd go with her.'

'Me…?' Liza loved her nan, her father's mother, a gentle, cheerful woman with a spine of steel. 'But I don't even know if I can take time off, Mum…'

'I'm sure you can and, in any case, it's only for a week in May. I can't go, with Lindsay's exams and Marie still at home, and besides, your nan can only stand me for about ten minutes. I know I'm too silly for her.'

Her mother spoke in her usual matter-of-fact way, but this time it made Liza's eyes fill with tears. 'You're not silly, Mum.'

'Oh, yes, I am. I'm a silly old bird, all right, and I don't mind. But your nan likes your company, and you've always wanted to see something of Europe. Now's your chance.'

'Europe? Where is she going?'

'A tour of Italy. She's got it all arranged and booked. All we need to do is book you a ticket, and make sure your passport hasn't expired. I know you haven't had any real cause to use it, but now's your chance.'

Italy… It was ridiculous to think she'd bump into Fausto in all of Italy, and yet still the prospect made her heart beat faster. 'I don't know, Mum…'

'You're going,' Yvonne said firmly. 'It'll be good for you, Liza. A change of scenery from all the grey we've been having. You need your spirits lifting.'

It was all arranged within a matter of days, and just a few weeks later Liza found herself on a flight to Milan with her nan, and then booked into a lovely little *pensione* on the shores of Lake Maggiore.

It was all so beautiful—the bougainvillea tumbling from pots on the little wrought iron balcony outside her window, the lake a deep, dazzling blue-green in the distance, the air warm and scented with lavender and thyme.

Her nan, Melanie, had informed her on the flight over that they would not be having a tour of the entire country, but rather one just of the Italian lakes.

'I've always wanted to see them, and as we only have a week we can hardly see everything in all of Italy.'

'I suppose not,' Liza agreed as a wave of trepidation—and surely not anticipation or even *hope*—went through her. Fausto's estate was, she knew, in the lakes region. Still, it was very, very unlikely that she would stumble upon him during their week-long stay. So unlikely it bordered on absurd, if not downright fantastical.

'So,' Melanie announced as she came into Liza's room, 'I thought we'd have dinner at the little restaurant down the street, and then tomorrow I want to take a tour of one of the estates nearby—some of its gardens are open to the public, along with a few of its main rooms. It's meant to be one of the most impressive properties in all of Europe.'

'Oh?' Liza asked. Then some towering sense of inevitability prompted her to go on, even while she already felt she knew, 'Who does it belong to?'

'The Conte di Palmerno,' Melanie said with a grand flourish. 'Apparently, he's someone quite important.'

* * *

The next morning dawned bright and sunny, and Liza tried to still the swarm of butterflies that had taken residence in her stomach as she took particular care with her appearance.

'You are not going to see him,' she scolded her reflection. 'He's probably not even in Italy, or if he is he'll be in Milan, working.' She took a deep breath as she smoothed her hands down the daisy-sprigged sundress she'd chosen to wear. 'Even if he's on the estate, it's completely unlikely that he'll be out wandering in the gardens when we are. So stop worrying.'

Except she didn't think she was worrying, precisely. *Hoping* was closer to the mark, which was an alarming realisation. Worry would be far more reassuring.

It was a twenty-minute cab ride to Villa di Palmerno, a beautiful drive along the shores of Lake Maggiore, with villas perched on the verdant hillsides and motorboats speeding along the calm blue waters.

'Stop fidgeting,' Melanie said with a laugh as next to her Liza shifted nervously and then checked her hair. 'We're just going to see some gardens.'

'I know,' Liza murmured, flushing, and once again she had to give herself a stern mental talking-to.

A few minutes later the taxi turned into the impressive wrought iron gates that led to the Palmerno estate. Liza drew her breath in at the sight of the endless smooth green lawns, the extensive gardens behind high stone walls and then the house—oh, the house.

She stared in wonder at the villa, with its balconies and balustrades, its turrets and terraces. Well over two dozen windows sparkled in the sunlight as the cab pulled up in front of the separate entrance to the vast gardens.

'Isn't it magnificent?' Melanie exclaimed, and Liza could not find it in herself to reply. When Fausto had been asking her to marry him, he'd been asking her to be mistress and chatelaine of all this. It was too awesome a thought to comprehend and in fact she hadn't comprehended it at all when she'd thrown his proposal back in his face.

She cringed now as she remembered just how thoroughly and thoughtlessly she'd refused him. *Absolutely, unequivocally no.* She closed her eyes and her heart against the memory as she got out of the car on weak, wobbly legs.

The gardens were beautiful, each one perfectly landscaped and surrounded by a high hedge to give privacy. They wandered through rose gardens and wildflower meadows, gardens with marble fountains and benches and gardens with trellises of wisteria and beds of lavender. They found a kitchen garden that was an acre at least, full of vegetables and seedlings. There was an orchard with every kind of fruit tree imaginable and half a dozen greenhouses where, a gardener informed them, the estate produced all sorts of tomatoes, melons and other fruits, including a unique orange that the Conte had helped to develop.

'What sort of man is the Conte?' Liza forced herself to ask in as casual a tone as she could, and the elderly gardener's lined face crinkled into a smile.

'He is *bene—molto bene!*' He kissed his fingers and then laughed. 'A very good master of the house, *signorina*. Truly the best. Some say he can be a bit reserved, but only those who do not know him truly. He is as kind and generous a man as anyone could wish.'

'I see,' Liza said, the words practically choking her, and she turned away.

Everything about the place, from the beautiful, endless gardens to the villa perched above them as gracious and lovely a building as one could ever imagine, not to mention utterly enormous, made Liza ache—not with longing for the material wealth she saw all around her, although it was unbelievably impressive.

She ached because of how quickly and completely she'd dismissed Fausto's claims about his family, his position. She'd considered them utterly unimportant, a matter not worth spending a second of thought on, and yet now she saw how understandable his concerns were.

He was lord of this place, responsible for hundreds, if not thousands, in his employ. He had a reputation to uphold, people's livelihoods to support, and naturally he would want a woman at his side who was capable of helping him shoulder such a huge responsibility, who could offer advice and welcome people from all walks of life, attend dinner parties and charity galas and press conferences and who knew what else. Of course he had to be cautious when thinking of his bride, his wife.

Yet she'd scorned it all in a moment of prideful pique. She'd scorned *him*, and now she found she deeply regretted it—regardless of his proposal or whatever future they might have had together, Fausto had deserved her to take him and his concerns seriously, rather than scornfully, and now it was too late. The bitter regret she felt was enough to choke her. She could have lain down right there in the garden and wept.

* * *

Fausto drove up and parked his navy sports convertible in front of the villa, the wind ruffling his hair as he gazed at his family home. It was good to be back; it was good to be away from London.

The last two months had crawled by, as he'd pulled sixteen-hour working days, returning to his Mayfair townhouse to simply eat and sleep. Even then he had not been able to banish thoughts of Liza—Liza, who had yielded so sweetly to him, who had rejected him so utterly. *Liza.* Why could he not forget her?

He wanted to, heaven knew. He'd even sent a reckless email to Gabriella Di Angio, a member of another of Lombardy's noble families, in order to re-establish an old connection. When she'd emailed back a blithe reply to tell him of her recent engagement to a French CEO, he'd only felt relieved. He did not want to renew his acquaintance with such a suitable woman. And yet he needed to stop thinking about a woman who was most unsuitable—a woman who didn't want him.

There had been plenty of opportunity to forget Liza in London. He'd gone out with Chaz several times, but his friend had been as dour as he was and neither of them had had any interest in the many women who'd sent all the right signals, and received none in reply.

With a sigh, Fausto stepped out of the car. Perhaps things would be better here, at Villa di Palmerno. At least he was further away from Liza, from temptation, from terrible, tempestuous memory.

He turned, and his heart seemed to still in his chest as he saw Liza herself walking through the garden gates with an older woman. For a few seconds he couldn't make any sense of it. How on earth could she be here? It was a figment of his imagination, a fantasy of his fevered mind...

But then she looked up and her eyes widened with shock and he knew it was her. She was here in the flesh, at Villa di Palmerno, just as he'd once imagined, bringing her back as his bride.

Slowly, wonderingly, Fausto took a step towards her. Liza froze where she stood, her gaze transfixed on his face, her expression wary, even frightened. Considering how they'd last parted, he could understand her uncertainty and yet suddenly, amazingly, it all seemed so simple to him, so very easy. She was here; he wanted her here. That was all that mattered.

'Liza.' He walked towards her, both hands extended, and she stared at him in blank wonder as he took her hands in his, gave them a light squeeze and then kissed her cheek. He inhaled her light floral fragrance and it reminded him of so much—but he couldn't think about all that now.

'Fausto,' she said faintly, 'I had no idea you would be here...'

'And I had no idea you would be here,' he returned with a smile. 'How did it come to pass?'

'You know him?' the older woman said in surprise, and then recollected herself. 'But obviously you do.' She held out her hand. 'Melanie Benton. I am Liza's grandmother.'

'Fausto Danti, Conte di Palmerno. Charmed to meet you,' Fausto said, and took her hand.

'Likewise.' Melanie looked both intrigued and pleased. No doubt she was wondering just what the nature of Fausto's relationship was with her granddaughter—as was he.

'My nan wanted to…to do a tour of the lakes,' Liza explained, stammering a little. 'And I came along to accompany her. I really had no idea you'd be here. I didn't even know we were coming here to the villa until last night…'

'It's a delightful surprise.' She looked shocked as well as dubious at his pronouncement, but Fausto meant every word. He was so very glad to see her. And she looked wonderful—her wild curls pulled back with a green ribbon, her sunglasses pushed up on her head. The sundress she wore was covered in daisies and her bare shoulders were tanned and sprinkled with golden freckles. He wanted to kiss every one. He wanted to kiss her—to take her in his arms, to feel her body against his, to tell her he didn't care about anything that had happened before.

The last two months had not lessened his feelings for Liza Benton in the least, he realised. They'd only grown stronger. And yet…he knew he needed to caution himself. As pleased as he was to see her, he had no intention of repeating his marriage proposal. One scorching rejection was certainly enough, if not one too many, especially considering he'd thought he'd already learned that unpleasant lesson before.

No, Fausto decided as he met Liza's enquiring gaze, he would have to proceed very cautiously—for his own sake as well as hers. He was glad she was here, but that was all. He wasn't ready to let it be more.

'We were actually about to leave,' Liza said, brandishing her phone. 'I was just going to call a cab.'

'Have you seen inside the house yet?' Fausto asked.

'No, I was hoping to see some of the rooms you have open to the public,' Melanie interjected, 'but I think Liza is a bit tired.'

Liza slid her gaze away from Fausto's and did not reply.

'Why don't you come into the house?' he suggested. 'I'll show you the public rooms myself, and then we can have some refreshments in the private apartments afterwards.'

'We couldn't—' Liza began, but Melanie was already nodding her vigorous acceptance.

'That is so very kind of you, Conte—'

'Please, call me Fausto.'

'Fausto.' She looked delighted. 'I really did want to see those rooms.'

Smiling at them both, Fausto ushered them into the villa. His mother was in Milan on a shopping trip, and Francesca was visiting friends. They had the house to themselves, and he was glad.

'Oh, lovely,' Melanie breathed as they stepped into the enormous entrance hall, with its black and white marble floor and skylight three storeys above. Liza regarded her surroundings silently, making no comment. Fausto couldn't keep from glancing at her, wanting to know what she thought. How she felt.

'Come this way,' he murmured, and he dared to put his hand on Liza's lower back for a brief instant before he removed it and ushered them towards the villa's main drawing room, a chamber of impressive proportions, with many antiques and rare works of art.

Melanie exclaimed over everything as he took them

through the drawing room, dining room, ballroom and library, but Liza said not a word. Fausto kept glancing at her to gauge her reaction, but her face was utterly expressionless. What was she thinking? And, more importantly, what was she feeling? He longed to know.

Having finished with the public rooms, he led them back to a sun-filled conservatory filled with plants and flowers that overlooked a wide terrace that led down to the villa's more private gardens.

'Oh, what a view!' Melanie exclaimed, for the shores of Lake Maggiore were glinting at the bottom of the gardens, jewel-bright. Villa di Palmerno had more lake frontage than any other lakeside property in Italy.

Fausto had rung for refreshments as soon as they'd started their tour, and they had only just sat down in comfortable rattan chairs in the conservatory when a maid brought in a tray with fresh lemonade, a selection of Italian pastries and a bowl of fresh fruit.

'Oh, you're so kind,' Melanie exclaimed. 'Really, Conte—Fausto. And I haven't yet asked…' She glanced thoughtfully at her granddaughter. 'How is it that you two know each other?'

Fausto leaned back in his chair, crossing one leg over the other as he glanced at Liza's sudden expression of alarm. After her deliberately blank looks all through their tour, it felt as if her careful veneer was finally cracking.

'Yes, Liza,' he said pleasantly. 'Why don't you explain to your grandmother how it is we know each other?'

CHAPTER THIRTEEN

LIZA FELT AS if she'd stumbled into some incredible alternate reality. Surely she couldn't be here, sipping lemonade and nibbling delicious pastries in Fausto Danti's amazing villa, while the man himself sat across from them, looking mind-bogglingly relaxed and acting so very charming? It felt impossible and yet it was happening, and she was here, and so was Fausto.

When she'd seen him step out of his car, some part of her hadn't even been surprised. Some part of her—a hopeful, desperate, wanting part—had *known* she would see him here. That secret part of her had been waiting for him all along and when she'd seen him a voice inside her had whispered thankfully, *At last*.

But what she hadn't expected was for Fausto to be so welcoming. His smile was easy, his manner assured, every word and gesture nothing but friendly. Yet the last time they'd met he'd been in a fury—and so had she.

What had changed? Why had he? Was it that he didn't care any more, and so such kindness was easy? Liza had no answers to any of it, but as she took a small sip of lemonade she knew she felt very, very cautious.

'Liza, aren't you going to explain?' Melanie asked with a laugh. 'How did you and Con—Fausto meet?'

'Well…' Liza licked dry lips as she took another nibble of her pastry, simply to stall for time. Outside, the verdant gardens tumbled down to the shining lake; she didn't think she'd ever seen anything so beautiful before. 'We met in a bar, actually.' Melanie's eyebrows rose and Liza clarified quickly, 'It was when Mum and Lindsay were visiting. Fausto was there with his friend and we all got to talking.' She glanced at him to see how he would take this explanation, and he nodded and smiled.

'Yes, and we met a few more times after that, didn't we?' His grey, glinting gaze met hers in laughing challenge, and in a panic she wondered why he was doing this. *Taunting* her.

'Yes, a few times,' she murmured. 'At a party…'

'And in Norfolk,' Fausto supplied. 'At the house of a mutual friend. My godfather, in fact. We had a lovely walk on the beach.' When Liza risked a glance at him she found he was gazing straight at her, and there was knowledge in his eyes. She felt herself flush as memories she'd been doing her best not to think about rose up in a rush. The kiss that had gone on and on…the feel of him against her…his body pressed to hers…

'I'm amazed you never said a word, Liza,' Melanie scolded. 'Considering you knew where we were going.'

'It…er…didn't seem relevant,' Liza said. She knew she sounded ridiculous. If she'd been more sophisticated and sanguine, she would have mentioned to her grandmother before about knowing Fausto in a careless manner, but she'd known she couldn't talk about him without revealing the depth of her emotion. It was hard enough now to act indifferent. In fact, it was impossible.

She didn't think she could sit here a moment more, pretending she and Fausto were nothing but casual acquaintances. She lurched upright, spilling a bit of her lemonade as she replaced it on the tray. 'It's getting late, Nan, and I'm sure the Conte is busy. We should get going.' She fumbled for her phone. 'I'll call a cab.'

'Nonsense, I'll have one of my staff drive you,' Fausto replied. 'It is no trouble. But I insist you return for dinner. Tomorrow night?'

Liza gaped at him while Melanie smoothly accepted the invitation. 'That would be lovely, thank you.'

'I don't think…' Liza began helplessly, knowing it was already too late. *Why are you doing this?* She tried to form the question in her eyes but Fausto either didn't see it or chose to ignore it.

'Let me arrange your transportation,' he said, and rose fluidly from his seat. As he left the room Melanie leaned towards Liza.

'What a lovely man,' she said in a hushed voice. 'I can't help but feel there's more to your knowing each other than you're willing to admit.'

'There isn't,' Liza replied woodenly. Nothing she wanted to relate to her grandmother, in any case.

'The car will be ready shortly,' Fausto said as he returned to the room. 'While we wait, perhaps I can show you the villa's private gardens?'

'That would be lovely,' Melanie said before Liza could frame a response.

Fausto opened the French windows that led onto a

wide marble terrace. Silently, Liza followed him, while Melanie exclaimed over everything.

Steps lined with flower pots ran all the way down the landscaped hill to the lake, and Fausto led them down while Liza trailed a little behind.

As they progressed down the hill he urged Melanie forward to look at the rose bushes while he dropped back a little to walk with Liza.

'I trust you are well?' he asked quietly.

'Yes.' Liza didn't trust herself to say anything else. Having him standing so close to her, looking so unbearably handsome in his navy blue suit, was just about all she could handle. Had his hair always been so dark, his jaw so hard, his body so powerful? Yes, she was sure it all had, and yet she felt herself responding in such an overwhelmingly visceral way to him now that it took all her strength not to reach out and touch him.

'I spoke to Henry back in March,' Fausto continued, his voice pitched low so Melanie wouldn't overhear their conversation. 'I wanted to make sure you were…well.'

It took her a moment to realise he meant *not pregnant*. She swallowed. 'That must have put your mind at ease.'

'It did, for your sake.'

She glanced at him sharply; as usual she couldn't tell anything from his expression. 'And not yours?'

'Such an…occurrence would have complicated matters, undoubtedly,' he replied after a brief pause. 'But I would not have regretted it.'

Which made her feel more confused than ever. 'That wasn't the impression you gave me the last time we met.'

'The impressions we gave each other were both unfavourable,' Fausto replied and Liza fell silent. She could not make sense of him at all. As they came onto the shore of the lake she realised she would have preferred him to be his usual self—cold and autocratic.

It would have made it so much easier for her heart to heal. As it was, she felt only confused and unhappy by his seeming solicitude. It didn't make *sense*. She'd thought him one sort of man, and now she was realising more and more that he might be another, and she did not know how to deal with either. Part of her wished she had never seen him again, even as another, far greater part yearned for him still.

'This is so very beautiful,' Melanie exclaimed yet again as they came onto the wide dock where a top-of-the-line speedboat was moored. 'I don't think I've ever seen such a pretty spot.'

'It is lovely,' Liza said, because she felt she had to say something. All of it—the blue, blue lake, the fringe of grey-green mountains on the horizon, the gracious villa and its gardens—was stunning, and looking at it all made her ache in a way she didn't want to examine too closely.

'Perhaps tomorrow we could go out in the boat,' Fausto said with a nod towards the craft in question. 'Then you would be able to see the lake properly.'

'I'm afraid I'm not one for being out on the water,' Melanie answered with a laugh. 'But I know Liza would enjoy it.'

'Then it shall be done,' Fausto said, and Liza gave him a quick, sharp look.

'I'm not one for boats either,' she said quickly. 'And

Nan and I were going to tour one of the other lakes to-morrow.'

'We don't—' Melanie began, but Liza shook her head.

'I want to.'

Fausto slanted her a wry, knowing look. 'Perhaps another time,' he said.

They walked back up to the villa and Liza made sure to walk ahead with her grandmother so Fausto couldn't speak to her again. His veiled references to their past stirred up far too much inside her. She didn't know how to respond to any of it. Was he being genuine? Or was he taunting her, showing her all that she could have had, but refused? She wouldn't even blame him if he was.

Perhaps he was doing both. One thing Liza knew was that Fausto's motives weren't clear, perhaps not even to himself. Perhaps he was, as he always was, fighting his attraction to her, because of her glaringly obvious un-suitability. At this point Liza didn't know if she could fault him for it. *She* didn't think she was suitable.

A few minutes later Fausto was escorting them out to the waiting luxury sedan, and he shook Melanie's hand before turning to Liza with an inscrutable smile.

'Until tomorrow evening.'

Was that a promise—or a threat? *What did he want from her?* Liza merely nodded, not trusting herself to speak. She got in the car and as it sped down the drive she forced herself not to look back, as much as she wanted to.

'So who is this woman, Fausto?'

Francesca's smile was teasing as she came into

Fausto's bedroom. He was standing in front of the mirror, adjusting the cuffs of his dress shirt, frowning slightly at his reflection.

'She's an acquaintance—a friend—from London.'

'A *friend*? She sounds rather special.'

Fausto spared his sister a smiling glance. 'You have always been a romantic, Chessy,' he said, using the nickname he'd given her in her childhood. Although she was nineteen years younger than him, an unexpected blessing after years of infertility for his parents, they'd always been close. Francesca had looked up to him, and he had doted on her. He didn't think that would ever change.

'I am a romantic,' Francesca allowed, 'but, you know, your voice changes when you speak of her.'

Fausto regarded his sister with a frown. 'It does not.'

'It does, Fausto,' she answered with a laugh. 'And the fact that you don't even know it, *and* that you deny it, makes me think she must be *really* special.'

Fausto decided not to deign his sister's observation with a reply. She was always seeing hearts and flowers where there were none, and in the case of Liza Benton...

What did he feel? Nothing as uncomplicated as simple romance or affection, he acknowledged as he turned away from the mirror. In fact, he had no idea what had motivated his extraordinary invitation yesterday. Yes, it had been the simple pleasure of seeing her again— but had there been something more? A desire to deepen their so-called friendship, or a more unflattering compulsion to let her see the full extent of all she'd missed out on?

Everything felt tangled, and yet nothing had really

changed. He still meant what he'd told her back in Norfolk—he had no intention of repeating his proposal.
He would not risk the kind of blistering rejection she'd
given him the first time around. If that made him as
proud as she'd accused him of being, then so be it.

'We should go downstairs,' he told Francesca. 'Our
guests will be here soon.' His mother was in Milan until
the weekend, which was just as well because he knew
she would not find Liza suitable in the least. His mother
was inherently proud, her dignity bordering on a reserve far chillier than anything Fausto had ever shown
Liza or anyone else. He did not look forward to the two
of them ever meeting, and perhaps they never would.

Downstairs, Fausto paced the drawing room, feeling
more restless than he wished as he anticipated Liza's
arrival. Already he was more than half regretting his
invitation. How would they bridge the tension and awkwardness that existed between them? Francesca was
sure to guess something of what had happened, if Liza's
grandmother hadn't already. She'd seemed like a rather
shrewd woman.

More importantly, he wished he had an understanding in his own mind of his feelings towards Liza Benton. As always, he felt pulled in two very different
directions—a deep and even consuming desire to be
with her, and a compulsion to push her away. She was
not a suitable bride for him or his family, a fact that
seemed even more obvious now that she was in his
surroundings.

And yet…and yet…she was lovely, and kind, and
gracious and smart—all very *suitable* qualities.

None of that mattered, however, Fausto reminded

himself, because Liza had refused him once and he would not risk such a bitter refusal again. A man could take only so much rejection, especially when it had been given with such scathing vehemence. So, really, all of this was utterly moot, and he'd treat her as he saw her—a casual acquaintance, someone he might call a friend. That was all. That was all it ever could be.

'I think they're here,' Francesca said excitedly, and Fausto felt his heart flutter, a most unusual and irritating sensation. He straightened, eyes narrowing as Paolo, the villa's butler, went to answer the door. A minute later he was ushering Liza and her grandmother into the private drawing room reserved for family and guests.

The first thing Fausto noticed was how sophisticated she looked. She wore a flowing jumpsuit in emerald-green silk and her hair was pulled back in an elegant up-do, a few curls escaping to frame her lovely face. She'd paired the outfit with a pair of chandelier earrings and high heeled sandals and he realised, with a warm glow of masculine admiration, that she could rival any of the socialites in his circle for both sophistication and beauty.

'Thank you for having us,' Melanie said, while Fausto found he could not tear his gaze away from Liza.

'It is my pleasure, I assure you,' he promised Melanie as he continued to look upon Liza. Under his lingering gaze a blush touched her cheeks and made her only look lovelier. Then he felt someone else's eyes on him and he turned to see Francesca looking at him with avid interest. 'Let me introduce my sister,' he said, and made the necessary introductions.

Soon Melanie was asking about the history of some of the artwork and while Fausto answered he saw, out of the corner of his eye, that Francesca and Liza were chatting away. A burst of laughter emerged from their bent heads and he wondered what on earth they were talking about. They were certainly getting along, and that knowledge was both unsettling and gratifying, giving him even more of a sense of the push-pull he'd always felt with Liza.

Dinner passed more easily and with more enjoyment than Fausto had expected. Liza was a sparkling conversationalist and although she mostly addressed her comments to Melanie or Francesca she would occasionally favour him with a remark or cautious smile.

Melanie asked about various aspects of the estate, which Fausto was happy to give. 'In fact,' he said halfway through the meal, 'you are drinking Danti wines. We have a vineyard as part of the estate, a few miles away.'

'What don't you have?' Liza said with a hint of laughter in her voice, although there was a serious question in her eyes that Fausto didn't know how to answer.

You, he thought unwillingly. *I don't have you.*

After dinner they retired to the drawing room for coffee, and Liza had just sat down when Francesca asked Melanie if she'd like to see the portrait gallery upstairs.

'You've been asking about our ancestors,' she said with a smile, 'so let me show you their faces.'

'Oh—' Liza started to get up but Francesca waved her aside. 'Why don't you stay here and keep Fausto company, Liza? He doesn't want to see those fusty old portraits again.'

And before Liza could even manage a reply they

were gone. Fausto smiled in bemusement; his sister's ploys were all too obvious. He glanced at Liza, who met his enquiring look with a wry smile of her own. Then she laughed.

'Are you thinking what I'm thinking?' he asked as he handed her a coffee.

'That your sister likes to play matchmaker?'

'She is a romantic. She can't help herself.'

'Does she know—about us?' Liza asked abruptly, the smile dropping from her face. 'I mean…what happened?'

Fausto took a sip of his coffee as he watched her expression turn wary and guarded. 'No, she does not. I have not told anyone about that.'

'Of course you haven't,' Liza agreed, and he raised his eyebrows.

'Your meaning…?'

She shook her head. 'Only that you wouldn't want people to know.'

'Only because I would not want anyone to know my private business, or yours, for that matter.' He searched her face, trying to discern her mood, but she rose from her seat and paced the room, her back to him as she sipped her coffee and looked out at the darkened gardens.

'Your villa—the whole estate—is very beautiful.'

'Thank you,' he said after a pause.

'I don't think I…realised what it was like when you spoke about it back in England.'

'It would be hard to imagine, I suppose.'

'It's more than that, but…' She let out a soft sigh. 'It doesn't matter now.'

He longed to ask her what she meant, yet some instinct kept him from pressing. This conversation already felt dangerous, flirting with emotions and memories he needed to suppress. As charming as Liza had been tonight, it was very clear that she was still keeping her distance, and Fausto knew he could not presume that anything between them had changed. He certainly had no intention on acting on such a presumption.

Liza's back, slender and tense, was still to him. The shadows lengthened in the room and the silence between them turned hushed, expectant. It would be so easy, so wonderful, to cross the few feet that separated them. So tempting to trail a fingertip down the bare expanse of her back, to hook a finger under the spaghetti strap of her jumpsuit and slip it off her golden, sun-kissed shoulder. Then he would bend his head and brush his lips against that spot, before moving even lower…

Fausto must have made some sound, some indication of his frustrated desire, for Liza turned suddenly, the coffee cup clattering in its saucer.

'I should go.'

'There's no need—'

'It's late, and we have an early start tomorrow. We're travelling to Lake Como and back all in one day.'

'How long are you staying in the area?'

'Till Wednesday.'

'Then you can come to our garden party this weekend.'

She shook her head as she looked at him miserably. 'Is that really a good idea, Fausto?' she asked quietly.

'Why wouldn't it be?'

'You've already made your point. I don't… I don't need to see any more. Experience any more. I get it.'

'What point is it I'm meant to have made?' Fausto asked, his tone sharpening, but before Liza could reply—not that Fausto was sure she would—Francesca came into the room, followed by Melanie.

'We've seen all the rellies,' Francesca said with a laugh. 'Some of them are so stuffy-looking it's ridiculous.'

'I was just telling Liza that she and her grandmother must come to our garden party this weekend,' Fausto told her sister. Francesca perked right up as he'd known she would, and turned to Liza.

'Oh, yes, do come. It's a tradition we have every year, to say thank you to all the staff and employees. It's so much fun—please say you'll come.'

Liza threw Fausto an accusing look before she smiled at Francesca and said stiffly, 'Of course, we'd love to. Thank you.'

Fausto could not deny the primal satisfaction that roared through him. He would see Liza again—and who knew what would happen between them then?

CHAPTER FOURTEEN

LIZA COULD HARDLY believe she was back at Villa di Palmerno again, this time for the garden party Fausto had more or less strong-armed her into. Once again reluctance warred with excitement, hope with fear. Seeing him was torture because it reminded her of how attracted she was to him and, more than that, how much she enjoyed his company. How easy it would be to let herself fall in love with him.

Yet she knew just from looking at Fausto that he had no intention of repeating his proposal, or re-establishing their relationship, not that what they'd experienced was even remotely close to that. Still, it had been the most important experience of Liza's life. She was still trying to get over it.

Even if she didn't understand Fausto's motivations for approaching her, she sensed that same reserve within him that had always been there, like a brick wall built against her, and it seemed to go deeper than his understandable concern about her suitability. She recalled his guarded remark back in Norfolk about another woman—was Fausto guarding his heart, the way she had? Too afraid to take a risk again?

In any case, Liza knew she did not have it in her to bring that wall down brick by brick, and he did not seem inclined to do so either. Guarded hearts or proud ones—what did it matter? The result was the same.

As they arrived at Villa di Palmerno the entrance was festooned with bunting and fairy lights and balloons of every colour arched over the villa's magnificent and ancient doorway. Francesca was waiting by the door to greet them, dressed in a plain white shirt and black skirt.

Liza have must looked surprised by her choice of outfit because Francesca laughed. 'Don't look so shocked—I'm dressed as a waitress. Every year when we throw a party for all the staff, all the Dantis do the waiting and serving. There's not enough of us, of course, so we have to bring in people as well—even my mother does her part.'

'And Fausto?' Liza asked sceptically. She could not picture him lowering himself in such a way.

'Oh, yes, he does as well,' Francesca said. 'It was his idea, actually—the tradition only started about five years ago.' She made a face. 'I don't think my father would have considered such a thing, but he was willing for Fausto to make his mark.'

Yet another facet to Fausto that she had not seen before—not been willing to see. 'It sounds fun,' Liza said.

'Go, have a look!' Francesca gestured to the gardens, which were crowded with people. 'There's lots of things to do.'

As Liza wandered around the gardens with her grandmother, she was amazed at every turn at all the festivities that had been arranged—there were carnival games of all kinds and stalls selling everything from plants to toys to delicate wood carvings. On the lawn there was even a small Ferris wheel and clowns on stilts offering balloons to every delighted child. It was utterly magical and she kept turning in a circle, not knowing where to look next, amazed by it all.

Even more amazing, and more humbling, was the vociferous praise she heard from every corner. All the staff attending the party were friendly, and their love for their employer was impossible to deny.

He was a good man, the best man, so kind and generous and fair. There was nothing he wouldn't do for any of them—Liza only half understood the stories several people told her because of the language difference, but the gist was clear enough. Fausto helped them all, he put them before himself, he was wonderful.

Too wonderful, she thought disconsolately, for her. Melanie had become caught up with several women she'd met, and Liza took the chance to slip away. As lovely as the party was, she didn't know how much she could take of all the good humour bubbling up, the joy and wonder and praise…not when she was feeling lower and lower herself.

She slipped through a hedge into a small octagonal rose garden that was blessedly quiet, but still felt too close to all the party mayhem. A little wrought iron gate led to another garden, enclosed by high hedges, a shell-shaped fountain in its centre.

Alone, Liza breathed a sigh of both sorrow and relief. It had been such a happy day, so why did she feel so sad? Not sad, precisely, she told herself, more just…

melancholy. And she was afraid to examine its source too closely.

She sat on the edge of the fountain and ran her fingers through the water spraying from the marble shell in a graceful arc. It shouldn't hurt her so much that she'd discovered that Fausto Danti was a good man—proud, yes, but generous, kind and good-hearted. It should be a relief, because of course she'd rather he wasn't horrible. He wasn't the *snobbish, arrogant, rude and unlikeable* person she'd once declared him to be. He was anything but.

Liza let out a choked cry of dismay and bowed her head.

'You look like Venus on the half-shell.'

She stiffened at the sound of his voice, even though some feminine instinct had known he would come, or at least had hoped.

'Why do you always find me in secret places?' she asked, trying to keep her voice light, but it trembled. She forced herself to look at him; he stood in the entrance to the garden, dressed in a white shirt and black trousers, just like he had been the first time she'd met him. She'd thought the clothes like those of a waiter back then, and today he *was* acting as a waiter, and yet he was anything but. He was so much more.

Standing there, his steely gaze sweeping over her, he looked so handsome he made everything in her ache. The hooded brows…the hard line of his jaw…the lithe beauty and power of his body. She had to look away, afraid her yearning would be evident in her face.

'Why do you always go to secret places?' he asked, his voice a low thrum as he took a few steps towards her.

'I wanted to be alone.'

'Should I leave?'

'No.' Liza knew she didn't want him to. He deserved her apology, at least, as much as it would pain her to give it. 'I wanted to see you. Speak to you.'

'Oh?' Fausto sounded terribly neutral, and she wondered if he was worried she would make some melodramatic declaration. What woman wouldn't, after all she'd seen and heard today? But no. She wouldn't embarrass them both with such an unwanted sentiment.

'I wanted to thank you for today,' she said, trying not to sound stilted. 'And not just for today. For dinner the other night…and the refreshments and tour from before. You've really been so very kind.'

'It's been no trouble.'

'Yes, but…you really didn't have to.' She forced herself to continue, although her throat had grown painfully tight and every word hurt her. 'Especially… considering how we left things. The last time…in Norfolk.' She risked a glance at him but his face was blank. *Of course.* She had never been able to read him, and she wished she had some inkling as to his feelings— although perhaps she didn't. Perhaps she'd be horrified if she knew what he felt right now, about her. How little he felt.

He inclined his head. 'Whatever passed between us is in the past, Liza. It does not need to affect the present.'

'Yes.' Liza nodded, a bit too much. 'That's very gracious of you.' And even though she suspected—or at least she hoped—that he meant it kindly, those words hurt too. *The past was in the past.* She was just a friend, barely more than an acquaintance. Whatever had happened between them had been all too brief, and probably forgettable as well. *She* was the one who had given it so much importance, who had let it change her whole being, even as she'd fought against it and then thrown it back in his face.

Fausto took another step towards her. 'Why is it, then,' he asked, 'that you look so sad?'

Liza lowered her head so her hair fell forward to hide her face, the chestnut curls resting against her cheek, making Fausto itch to run his hand along her jaw, tuck those wayward curls behind her ear.

'I'm not sad,' she said after a moment, her head still bent.

'Are you sure?'

'I think I know what I'm feeling.' She spoke with humour rather than ire, and Fausto rocked back on his heels, unsure how to handle this moment, or what he wanted from it. The trouble was, he didn't know what *he* was feeling.

Part of him wanted to sweep away all the regrets and memories and simply take Liza in his arms. Forget everything else. Another part of him was wary, not wanting to risk rejection and hurt. And yet another part was trying to be wise, reminding that instinctive impulse that Liza still wasn't suitable, no matter how much she seemed so. Since he'd returned to Italy his mother had put on the pressure for him to find a bride. He had obligations, responsibilities, expectations. Yet that insistent voice was growing quieter and quieter with every moment he spent with this woman.

He strolled over to the other side of the fountain and

sat on its edge. In the distance he could hear the sound of the party, laughter and music, a background of joy.

'How have you been these last few months?' he asked. 'Really?'

'Okay,' she said. She ran her fingers through the fountain's water, still not looking at him. 'Ish.'

He hated the thought that he'd been the one to hurt her. He settled more comfortably on his perch. 'How is your family?'

'The same.' She sounded bleak rather than tart. 'It's amazing, what you've done here with the party,' she continued, clearly not wanting to talk about herself. 'Everyone I spoke to sang your praises.'

'They are good people.'

'You're a good person.' She looked at him for the first time, her eyes heartbreakingly wide. 'I want—I need—to say that, especially after all the things I accused you of, back in Norfolk. You aren't any of those things. I'm sorry I said you were.'

Her apology, so plainly stated, touched him deeply, and now he found he was the one who was looking away, to hide the depth of his emotion. 'I'm still proud,' he said, trying for wryness.

'You have a right to be proud, of who you are and all you've achieved. The people I talked to today told me how you have increased the business, watched out for their welfare, navigated them through difficult times. You are a wonderful employer, by all accounts. A wonderful Conte di Palmerno.' She spoke his title with an attempt at an Italian accent that made Fausto smile even as he ached. He hadn't expected this conversation to be so sweet—or so hard.

'Thank you, Liza.'

'I… I hope there are no hard feelings between us, after everything. Most likely we won't see each other after today, but still. I'd like to part on a good note.' She smiled, her lips trembling as they curved upwards, her glinting hazel eyes searching his face, looking for answers.

He was silent, unable to agree to the assumptions she'd made—that they wouldn't see each other again after today, that they would be saying their final goodbyes.

'Fausto…?' Her voice wavered with uncertainty.

'There are no hard feelings,' he said at last. 'Although I don't like to speak in so final a tone. Today doesn't have to be goodbye.'

'Well…' she shrugged, trying for another smile '…it sort of does, doesn't it? You're back in Italy. I'm in England. And our worlds do not…intersect.' She glanced around the garden, the shadows lengthening on the paving stones as the sky slowly turned to violet. 'I realise that now—how different we are. Our worlds, our… positions. I didn't really understand what you meant. I thought you were just being snobbish, until I came here and saw all this.' She swept one graceful arm to encompass the garden, the villa, the estate, even, he thought, his title. 'I shouldn't have been so scornful about your concerns. In my own way, I was proud too. I see that now.'

Fausto pressed his lips together, fighting an irrational desire to disagree with everything she'd just said. All the things he'd insisted mattered *didn't*, not in the way he'd thought, and not in the way she was now intimating. He didn't care about their *positions*. Heaven help him, how could he have said something so stupid?

'You weren't proud,' he said in a low voice.

'Well…it doesn't matter, does it? Any more.' She made it a statement rather than a question and, unable to argue with her because he had no promises he could make, Fausto stood up.

'Come back to the party. Now that it's getting dark we have a buffet dinner, followed by fireworks. Also, I would like you to meet my mother.'

'Your mother…?' Her expression showed nothing but alarm. 'I don't think…'

'I want you to meet her.' Why, he couldn't say, even in the privacy of his own mind. Viviana Danti, the Dowager Contessa, would be coolly polite to Liza, and no more. Definitely no more.

But perhaps *that* was why. Because he was hardly going to be dictated to by his mother, especially in something like this. *And as for your father…?*

The question reverberated through him hollowly, because he knew his esteemed father would have felt the same as his mother. *Honour is everything. Remember who we are… You have a duty…*

Don't make the same mistake again.

He had promised his father he would marry a suitable woman, after the disaster with Amy. A promise he'd always intended to keep, but now he wondered if it could look different. Liza might not be from the background his parents had wanted, but she certainly had all the qualities he'd look for in a wife. She wasn't Amy, not even close, and he felt far more for her than for a woman he'd convinced himself he was in love with fifteen years ago.

And yet…he'd made promises to his father, promises he'd had instilled in him since he was but a child, and ones he had always, always intended to keep. They'd defined him. But now he felt as if he were spinning in a sudden void, wondering about the bulwarks that had been his foundation.

'Fausto?' Liza regarded him uncertainly. 'I'm not sure it's a good idea to meet your mother.'

'It is,' he said firmly. 'Come with me, back to the party.' He held out his hand and Liza looked as if it were a foreign object. Then, after an endless few seconds, she put her hand in his. It was small-boned and slender, and he twined his fingers with hers, enjoying the feeling, as intimate as a kiss.

Silently, as if neither of them wanted to break the spell that was being woven over them, they walked from the garden, back to the party.

Dusk was falling softly, a violet cloak dropping over the world. Chinese lanterns were strung through the garden, creating warm pockets of light, and torches had been brought out to the terrace so it was flickering with shadows, an enormous buffet set up by the bank of French windows.

'I'll need to do my job in a moment,' he said, nodding towards the buffet. 'But after everyone is served, I'll introduce you to my mother.'

'Okay,' Liza said, still sounding unconvinced that this was a good plan.

'Come and eat,' Fausto said, and he led her to the buffet and gave her a plate before taking his position behind, as a server. He wished he could have stayed with her, but he knew he would never shirk his position. It was important that all the people who served him so unwaveringly saw him willing to serve them in some small way.

Still, he kept his eye on Liza as she moved down the buffet, a pensive look on her face. She looked so lovely, with her hair wild about her face, her broderie anglaise top matched with a pair of bright blue culottes. Casual yet elegant, a perfect choice for the day, and as he watched her chat to some of the vineyard workers, men with broken English and rough manners, with friendly ease, something warm and sure started in his chest and spread outward. He was glad she was here.

That feeling of gladness, of certainty, only increased as the evening progressed. As Fausto served and chatted, his gaze kept moving to Liza, tracking her around the terrace as she chatted to various people, always friendly and open.

His mother had been holding court in the drawing room for most of the evening, and Fausto decided their introduction could wait. He wanted Liza to himself.

When the buffet had finished he went to join her by the balustrade overlooking the lawn where the fireworks would be set off. 'I'm sorry I couldn't be with you,' he said as he came to stand by her side and she gave him a swift, searching look.

'It's all right.'

'You've been enjoying yourself?'

'Actually, yes.' She let out a little laugh. 'Everyone is so friendly.'

'You are easy to talk to.'

She let out another laugh, this one uncertain. 'Fausto, you're so full of compliments tonight. I don't know what to do with them.'

'Stay,' he said, the word like a pulse, and she gazed out at the darkened lawn, her body so very still. 'Please.'

The first fireworks went off, showering the sky with colour and casting her face in eerie light for a few seconds so he could see how pensive she looked.

'What do you mean exactly?' she asked, her voice unsteady.

'Stay here tonight. With me.'

Another Catherine wheel exploded in the sky, followed by applause and laughter.

'My grandmother…' Liza murmured, and triumph and desire roared through him. If that was her only objection…

'She can stay as well. I will make arrangements for a guest room to be made up. She must be tired. It would be better for her to be here.'

'And me?' Liza asked, turning to look at him, a look of such open vulnerability on her face that Fausto longed to take her in his arms.

'It is better for me,' he said quietly. 'If you stay. I want you to stay. But only if you want to.'

An age seemed to pass as firework after firework burst in the sky and Liza watched them, her expression both thoughtful and hidden. Then, finally, wonderfully, she turned to Fausto.

'Yes,' she said simply.

CHAPTER FIFTEEN

LIZA FOUGHT A sweeping sense of unreality as she and
Fausto watched the rest of the fireworks, side by side
and unspeaking. She couldn't believe what he'd asked
of her, or that she'd agreed. This was the last outcome
she'd expected, and yet some part of her acknowledged
the rightness of it. She was, amazingly, not surprised.

Neither was she naïve. One night. That was what
Fausto was asking of her. One night, and no more. She
pushed the thought away as soon as she'd had it; she
did not need to remind herself of how fleeting this one
night would be. And while it was happening she wanted
to savour every precious moment.

The sky darkened as the last sparks fell from it, and
people began to trickle towards the front of the villa
to go home. In the darkness Fausto gave her a swift
searching look.

'I must go and say my goodbyes.'

'Yes. I should find my grandmother…'

'My head of staff, Roberto, will assist you with anything you need.'

Liza didn't reply because she didn't know what as-
sistance she needed, or how she would find Roberto,

and part of her just wanted to take cover in the darkness. The *thought* of being with Fausto was far more compelling than the unbearably awkward logistics of making it happen.

He strode off to make his goodbyes, and Liza went in search of Melanie amidst the crowd of happy partygoers. It only took a few minutes to find her; her grandmother had been watching the fireworks on the terrace as well. When Liza explained the arrangements for the night Melanie's eyebrows rose but she acquiesced readily enough.

'I am tired. It will be good not to have to drive all the way back to the *pensione*.' She gave Liza a considering look. 'The Conte is very kind.'

'Yes.'

A man seemed to materialise out of the darkness, smooth and urbane. 'The Conte asked me to show you to your quarters, and make sure you have everything you need.'

'Oh…er…yes.' Liza couldn't help but be flustered. She felt as if her intentions—Fausto's intentions—were emblazoned on her forehead. Roberto, however, was discretion itself and he led Melanie to a sumptuous guestroom upstairs before taking Liza to hers.

'Ring this bell if there is anything you need,' he said, pointing to a buzzer by the door, and Liza nodded. Her heart had started thumping as soon as she'd entered the room—a spacious bedroom with a huge canopied king-sized bed taking pride of place. *What was she doing?*

The door clicked softly shut as Roberto left her alone. Liza paced the room nervously for a few minutes, before she decided she might as well avail herself of the huge walk-in shower in the en suite bathroom, as well as the thick terrycloth robe hanging on the door.

Twenty minutes later she was showered and swathed in the robe—and still alone. Had Fausto had second thoughts? What if this had all been some sort of a set-up? A payback for the humiliation she'd caused him with her insults and refusal?

But no. After everything she'd learned about him today, everything she knew, she could not believe such a thing of him.

The door opened.

Liza drew her breath in sharply as Fausto stood framed by the doorway, tall and dark and powerful. He regarded her silently for a moment and Liza let out an uncertain laugh, wishing she hadn't decided to don nothing but a robe. She'd been thinking only about not wanting to be hot and sticky, but now she was thinking about being naked.

'I wasn't sure if you would come, after all,' she said.

'Truthfully? I couldn't wait to get away.' His voice was low, and her heart fluttered. She did not reply because she didn't know how to. He took a step into the room. 'You haven't changed your mind?'

'No.' Her voice wavered and she set her chin. 'No,' she said more firmly.

'Good.' Fausto closed the door behind him, and instantly Liza felt as if they'd been cocooned. They were alone, truly alone, at last. Nervously she glanced around the bedroom, conscious again that she wore only a robe.

'This is a very beautiful room, but I imagine every room in this villa is just as beautiful.'

Fausto gazed around the room, his expression indifferent. 'The most beautiful thing in the room is you.'

Liza couldn't keep from giving a sceptical laugh as she shook her head. 'You don't have to soften me with compliments, Fausto. I'm already here.'

He frowned, his dark brows drawing together. 'Is that what you think I am doing?'

'Well…yes.'

'You are beautiful, Liza. I noticed that from the first moment that I saw you.'

'Now I know you're telling lies,' Liza returned lightly, even though it hurt. After all these months, after all that had passed between them, that first little dig still possessed a needle-like pain.

Fausto's frown deepened. 'What do you mean?'

'I heard you, that first night, by the bar. "She looked as plain and boring as the other, if not more so".' She tried for a smile. 'So don't pretend you were blown away by my beauty the first time you clapped eyes on me.'

'I said that?'

'Yes.'

'And you heard?'

'Yes.'

He sighed and shook his head. 'No wonder you took such a dislike to me right away. I did wonder.'

'You *were* rude.'

'Yes, I was. I was tired and I've never liked big social gatherings, but still there is no excuse. I'm sorry.'

Liza laughed and looked away, discomfited by the sincerity of his apology. 'I didn't tell you that to wheedle an apology out of you.'

'I *am* sorry,' Fausto said seriously. 'I never should

have said such a thing. If I thought it, it was only because I wanted to dismiss you, and I couldn't, even at the beginning.'

Which brought them to the very prickly nettle neither of them wanted to grasp. Even now, when they were alone together, when Fausto had asked her here, he would still dismiss her at some point. He would still want to. But hopefully not till the morning.

'Never mind about all that,' Liza said as she moved past him to the window, its shutters open to the night air, the gardens swathed in darkness below. 'It's all water under the bridge, anyway.'

'Is it?'

'Yes.'

'Good,' Fausto said after a pause. 'That is how I would like it to be.'

She nodded unsteadily, turning back to look at him, and he glanced towards the bathroom.

'Would you mind if I had a shower first?'

First. Before what? Liza fought an urge to laugh—hysterically. This was all so very much beyond her experience. 'No, of course not.' She gestured to the bathroom, with its marble and gold taps. 'Be my guest,' she quipped. 'Even though I'm yours.'

Fausto gave her a fleeting smile and then disappeared into the bathroom. A few seconds later Liza heard the sound of the shower. Her breath came out in a rush as she sagged with something like relief. This all felt so strange, and yet she *wanted* to be here. Even if only for a night.

Still, she had no idea how things were going to go when Fausto came out of the bathroom. What if he was naked? Where would she *look*? A muffled laugh escaped her and she clapped her hand over her mouth. Assured seductress she was not.

And yet… Fausto still wanted her. Had chosen her, at least for this. And whatever sorrow or heartache tomorrow and the days after might bring, at least she would always have tonight.

Liza hoped it would be a precious, even sacred, memory. She thought it might be. And, she acknowledged as she gazed out at the darkened night, it would have to be enough.

From the bathroom she heard the sound of the shower turning off.

Fausto slowly dried himself as he gazed unseeingly at the steam-fogged mirror. He could hardly believe that he was here…that she was here. When he'd asked her to stay the night it had felt both natural and essential. All he wanted.

And while he wasn't allowing himself to think too much about any possible future, the rightness of this evening, of them being together, burrowed down deep into his soul. It felt, in a way he could not explain even to himself, like their wedding night.

Wrapping the towel around his waist, he opened the bathroom door. Liza whirled around at the sound, her lovely eyes widening at the sight of him.

'Oh…' Her gaze swept up and down the length of his nearly naked body as a rosy blush reddened her cheeks. 'Oh,' she said again, softly this time, and with admiration.

'You seem nervous,' he remarked as he took a step towards her.

'Of course I'm nervous. You do realise the only other time I've done anything like this was on that beach?'

'I wondered if there had been anyone else since.'

'In the last two months?' Liza stared at him incredulously. 'Of course not.'

'You are a lovely woman,' he pointed out with a smile at her outrage. 'You must have admirers.'

'I work all day with an octogenarian,' Liza reminded him. 'And I haven't been going out very much. So no, there haven't been any *admirers*.'

'I'm glad.'

'Are you?' She looked at him seriously. 'You must have had…other women, in the meantime. I wouldn't mind, of course—'

'No.'

'No?' She looked surprised. 'But…'

'I've been working eighteen hours a day, hardly going out at night, and the truth is, I haven't wanted anyone else.' He was amazed at how freeing that admission felt. 'Only you.'

'Fausto…'

'Why don't you believe me?'

'I don't know. Because you're so amazing and I'm so…'

'You're so what?' he asked gently.

She let out an uncertain laugh. 'Plain. Boring. The sister who isn't pretty. The one people skip over, or simply forget.' Each word vibrated with an old, remembered pain and Fausto felt a flash of anger for the idiots who had dismissed her in such a way.

'You are none of those things, Liza. None.'

'I'm not amazing,' she said, clearly trying to sound merely wry.

'You are.' He reached for her hand, because he had to touch her. 'You are utterly amazing.' He brushed his lips against her fingers, and then he gently nibbled her fingertips as he kept his gaze on her, felt his own heat.

'You make me feel amazing,' Liza admitted unsteadily. 'In a way no one else ever has.'

'I'm glad for that too.'

'You're sounding very possessive,' she said with a breathy laugh.

'I'm feeling very possessive,' Fausto answered, and then he tugged on her hand so she came towards him, willing and expectant. Her hips bumped his and heat flared in them both. He felt it in himself as well as in her. She drew a shuddery breath and then, tentatively, placed her hands on his chest, spreading her fingers wide.

'Is that okay?' she asked a little anxiously. 'Can I touch you?'

'Oh, Liza,' Fausto said with a groan. 'You can touch me all you want. Anywhere.'

She laughed as she let her hands slip down his chest, her fingertips flirting with the edge of his towel before skimming up again.

'Go ahead,' Fausto encouraged her in a low, thrumming voice. Already he was more than ready for all she could give him. 'Touch me. Take off the towel.'

'Seriously?' An incredulous smile quirked her mouth.

'Seriously.'

Her hands travelled down again, her breath coming in a gasp as she tugged the towel and it fell away. She glanced down and her eyes widened comically.

'Oh…'

'Nothing to alarm you, I hope,' he said dryly.

'No…it's just I didn't actually *see* you, before.'

'And I didn't see you.' He reached for the sash of her robe and gave it a gentle tug. 'May I?' She nodded. He undid the sash and the robe parted, to reveal the shadowy valleys and curves of a body he ached to touch and treasure.

In one sinuous movement Liza shrugged the garment off and it fell in a heap at her feet. She kicked it away, chin raised, gaze defiant and yet vulnerable.

She was lovely…so lovely, her body pale and perfect, slender and supple. Fausto put his hands on her waist, nearly spanning it as he drew her towards him so their bodies brushed—her breasts against his chest, their hips nudging one another. She let out a shuddery breath and closed her eyes.

He tilted her chin up with one finger. 'All right?' he asked quietly, and she nodded.

'Yes. Very much so.'

'Good.' And then, because he couldn't wait any longer, he kissed her, and it was as sweet as it had been every time before—no, he realised, sweeter. It meant more, because he knew this—what was unspooling between them like a golden thread now—meant more. As he deepened the kiss his mind blurred and he let the thoughts drift away on a tide of sensation.

Liza put her arms around him and as their bodies came in even closer and more exquisite contact another groan escaped him. This was torture—wonderful, wonderful torture.

Stumbling a bit, they made it to the bed. Fausto pulled back the duvet as Liza moved over, her wild curls spread across the ivory pillowcase, her body and heart both open to him. Fausto stretched beside her and hooked one of her curls around his finger.

'Your hair,' he murmured, 'is magnificent.'

She let out another one of her disbelieving laughs. 'It's too curly.'

'Too curly? No. Why do you disparage yourself?'

'I don't know. I've never thought of it that way.' She shrugged slim shoulders. 'I know I've never been as pretty as Jenna, or as spirited as Lindsay, or as clever as Marie.'

'Marie? I haven't met her.'

'No, although you might like her the best. She's quiet and bookish.'

'I like *you* the best,' he said, and then he rolled over and covered her body with his own.

She let out a little gasp of pleasure before he devoured her mouth in a kiss and her arms came around him. She arched up into him, all pliant softness, and it was almost too much.

He kissed his way from her mouth to her breasts… breasts he could feel the ripe fullness of now, could touch and savour in a way he hadn't been able to in their frenzied rush on the beach. Now he would take his time, exploring every hidden curve, every sweet dip. He kissed his way lower.

Beneath him Liza writhed as she let out lovely little

mewling sounds of pleasure, her fingers raking through his hair as he kissed her soft thighs.

'Fausto…' she said shakily, half plea, half protest.

'I'm getting to know you,' he murmured, and she let out a breathless laugh as he kissed her at the core of herself and her body convulsed around him.

'Oh, I didn't *think*…'

'Now is not the time for thinking,' he advised. 'Only for feeling.' His mouth moved over her once more, and her body arched sweetly against him.

'*Fausto*…'

He could explore her hidden recesses for ever, but the desperate ache they both felt needed to be sated. They had the whole night in front of them, and he intended to use every single hour of it. But, for now, he reached for a condom.

'Are you ready?' he asked as he rolled on top of her once more, bracing himself on his forearms. Liza nodded, her head buried in his shoulder, her body open to him.

'Yes…*yes*.'

And she was, as he glided smoothly into her, found his way home, and she met him there, thrust for glorious thrust.

It was moments, and yet it was a lifetime shattered and reborn as she enfolded him in her body, clasped him in her arms, and they both broke apart and then came together. *This was where he wanted to be.*

All his concerns about positions or pride, all the armour he'd surrounded himself with to keep himself apart, to keep from gambling on that all-or-nothing risk of loving—it all shattered in this moment.

None of it mattered. None of it mattered in the least.

All he wanted was her. For tonight—and for ever.

He kept his arms around her as he rolled onto his back, their hearts thudding hard against one another in the aftermath of their lovemaking.

'That's just the beginning,' he promised her, and she pressed her forehead against his chest.

'You'll be the death of me.'

And yet, Fausto knew as he kept his arms around her, she was the life of him.

CHAPTER SIXTEEN

LIZA WOKE SLOWLY, blinking in the sunlight, stretching as languorously as the cat that got the cream. And that was how she felt after a night of gorgeous, mind-blowing and body-altering lovemaking.

She was sore in places she'd never been sore before and her muscles ached in a way that felt delicious. As she lay there in the sunlight, in the dreamy, muted state between sleep and consciousness, a montage of lovely memories danced through her mind. Candlelight on burnished skin. Fausto poised above her. His head bent as he kissed her, her fingers in his dark hair…

And then later, when she'd felt bolder, she'd given him the same sensual treatment. She'd explored every gorgeous inch of his lean, hard body and revelled in her newfound knowledge. They'd fallen asleep in each other's arms some time towards dawn.

Liza turned her head and saw Fausto sleeping next to her, his inky lashes fanned on his cheeks, his chest rising and falling in the steady beat of sleep.

And then, as consciousness crept in, so did reality. It was over. Her one amazing night had ended. And it had been amazing—she had no regrets. Well, not many.

198 PRIDE & THE ITALIAN'S PROPOSAL

The heartache she'd carry with her felt like a heavy yet necessary burden to bear, because she knew now that she loved him. How could she not, after all she'd learned about him? After everything he'd done for her, the kindness, sensitivity and passion he'd shown.

Of course she loved him.

And for a few precious seconds as she watched him sleep she imagined telling him so. She pictured how his face would soften in pleasure and surprise, and then he would take her in his arms and tell her he loved her too.

Of course it was only the stuff of fairy tales. In all the conversations they'd had since she'd come to Italy Fausto had never changed his position on position. On the fact that she was not suitable to be his bride—a fact Liza had felt more and more keenly, the more time she spent at Villa di Palmerno.

She was the Benton sister who had never been anything special, often overlooked or forgotten, one of many rather than a stand-out. She was the woman a man had sneeringly dismissed, had used just to get to her sister. Did she actually think she could be a *Contessa*?

No, of course not.

Slowly, Liza slipped out of bed, not wanting to disturb Fausto. Best if she showered and dressed, made her farewells as quickly as possible. Severed the connection as neatly and cleanly as she could, even if the thought of it hurt more than she could bear.

She'd just taken her clothes into the bathroom when her phone buzzed with an incoming text. Considering it was only seven in the morning, Liza frowned at the sound and swiped her screen. The text was from Jenna.

Are you awake? Need to talk.

Liza pressed 'call' and seconds later she heard Jenna's breathless voice. 'Liza? Sorry to wake you up so early...'

'It's fine, but it's only six in England. What's going on?'

'It's Lindsay,' Jenna said on a jagged note. 'We found out late last night... I didn't want to disturb you...but I couldn't wait any longer. Mum's having fits.'

Liza's stomach plunged icily. 'What's happened?'

'She's been so...oh, I can't even blame her, honestly. She's only just eighteen. Of course her head was bound to be turned.'

'What? Jenna, I have no idea what you're talking about.'

'Lindsay went to London for the weekend,' Jenna explained. 'You remember it's her eighteenth?'

'Yes...' Liza said, although she realised with a stab of guilt that, in light of everything that had been happening here with Fausto, she'd completely forgotten about her sister's birthday.

'Anyway, she told Mum she was seeing me, but she wasn't. She'd met some guy at a club the last time she was here—he invited her to some D-list party this weekend. Honestly, it sounded dire.'

'Oh, no,' Liza said softly. She could picture how thrilled Lindsay would be at such an invitation, how utterly irresponsible she might be at such an event, and also how out of her depth. Poor, foolish Lindsay.

'What happened?' she asked as dread swirled coldly in her stomach.

'I don't know the details, and I'm not sure I want to,' Jenna said with quiet grimness. 'She got involved with some minor celebrity at the party—I haven't heard of him, but Mum had.'

'And?' Liza asked, as everything in her went tenser.

'And there were photos involved. Nude photos.'

'Oh, no, Lindsay…'

'And the guy she was with, this Jack, is threatening to sell them to the tabloids—because this celebrity is apparently big enough for that—if we don't pay out.'

'Jack?' Liza knew even before she asked, 'Jack who?'

'Wick something, I think.'

'Wickley.' She closed her eyes. How could that wretched man be tormenting her family now? If she'd had any doubts about the truth of Fausto's story—and she hadn't—they would certainly have been swept away now.

'You know him?' Jenna asked in surprise.

'No, not really. It doesn't matter. What are we going to do?'

'I don't know. Mum's adamant the photos don't get published. She's worried for Lindsay's wellbeing, of course, but I also think she's afraid of her being expelled from school right in the middle of A-levels. They have a zero tolerance policy about this sort of thing.'

'And if she's expelled, no university,' Liza finished numbly. Despite her sister's seemingly scatty attitude, she had brains and she'd been offered a place studying business in Manchester.

'Her whole life could be derailed,' Jenna concluded miserably. 'Not to mention the humiliation and hurt she would feel. I know Lindsay acts shameless, but she isn't really. She's been reckless and silly, I know that, but she doesn't deserve this. She's trying to act as if she doesn't care, but I think she must.'

'Poor Lindsay.' Liza's mind was racing. 'I'll fly back today.'

'Oh, but your holiday—'

'It will be over in a few days, anyway. And this is more important.' Besides, Liza thought, her holiday already felt as if it were over. Her night with Fausto certainly was. 'I'll text you from the airport,' she promised, and then she disconnected the call.

She dressed quickly, her mind buzzing all the while, and when she emerged from the bathroom Fausto was sitting up in bed with a sleepy smile. Their night together already felt like something consigned to the past.

'Liza…' His smile vanished as he took in her agitation. 'What's happened?'

'Lindsay.' She couldn't keep it from him, as much as she wanted to. As she related the details of the sordid tale, she couldn't help but cringe inside. If there had ever been a measure of how unsuitable she was as his potential bride, now it was taken to the full, but that hardly mattered. She had to think about Lindsay, not herself.

'That bastard,' Fausto said in a low voice. 'He never tires of ruining lives.'

'I don't know what we'll do,' Liza said numbly. 'We can't afford to pay him. We haven't any money, not like that. But I have to go home and help. I need to be there for Lindsay, for Mum…'

Fausto was already getting out of bed and pulling on his trousers. Liza watched him miserably. Could he not get away from her fast enough, now that he knew the full extent of her family's shame?

'I'll arrange for a private flight for you back to England,' he said. 'It will be quicker.'

'Oh, you don't—'

'It's nothing,' he dismissed. 'Of course I will do it.'

'Thank you—'

'I will have it arranged.'

Liza blinked; Fausto's voice sounded so cold. Perhaps he was only offering because he wanted her out of here—out of Italy—as quickly as possible. He didn't even look at her as he buttoned his shirt, and Liza realised his mind was elsewhere; he'd already forgotten her.

Perhaps he was trying to do his own damage control. If Lindsay's photos ended up in the papers and Fausto's association with Liza was discovered she supposed it could reflect badly on the Danti family. She could hardly blame him for wanting to deal with the possible fallout for his own family, and yet the realisation filled her with sadness. Their one amazing night really was well and truly over.

Everything seemed to happen in super speed after that. Fausto left the bedroom without saying goodbye or even looking at her, and when Liza had finished getting ready and gone downstairs he was nowhere to be seen. His mother, Viviana Danti, however, was. Liza recognised her instantly even though they'd never met.

'I trust you had a comfortable night?' she asked in a glacial tone that made Liza freeze where she stood in the entrance hall. She'd just asked Roberto to find her grandmother and she was hoping to make her escape as quickly as possible.

'Yes.' Bravely, a bit recklessly, she stuck out her hand. 'I don't think we've met. I'm Liza Benton.'

'I know who you are,' Viviana Danti said coldly, ignoring Liza's hand. She withdrew it, blushing at the woman's icy hauteur.

'The party yesterday was lovely,' she said after a pause, because the silence was simply too awful. Viviana inclined her head.

'I understand you feel my son has developed some sort of attachment to you,' she said. 'Please don't think it will last.'

Stung, Liza replied, 'I never thought it would, but thank you for making it abundantly clear.'

Viviana smiled, a chilly gesture that held no friendliness. 'I am trying to help you, my dear. A girl such as yourself… It is understandable that you would have hopes.'

Until Viviana Danti had said it aloud, Liza wouldn't have believed she'd had such hopes. She'd reminded herself again and again that she didn't, that she'd walked into last night knowing full well that was all it could be.

And yet.

And yet…

Looking at Viviana's icy elegance, how she looked down her nose at her in the same way Fausto once had… Liza realised painfully that she'd been hoping all along. Hoping so hard, because how could she not, after last night? After how passionate Fausto had been. How tender.

'I have no such hopes,' she stated in as cold a voice as she could manage.

'Are you quite sure?' Viviana asked coolly. 'Because we have been in this situation before, you know. Fausto brought a girl home very much like you. Amy—young, English, poor.' She paused. 'It only took a more tempting offer to make her go away.'

Liza stared at her for a few stunned seconds before she said in a thready voice, 'Are you…are you offering me a bribe?'

'I'm giving you an incentive, along with a warning,' Viviana replied. 'I thought my son had outgrown such foolish fancies, but it appears he hasn't. How much will it take? Fifty thousand? A hundred?' She smiled coolly, and Liza took a stumbling step away. No wonder Fausto worried about gold-diggers. How much had this Amy taken?

'I have absolutely no wish to take a penny from you,' she said coldly. 'And don't worry, because I don't intend to see Fausto again.' The knowledge ripped through her and she drew a shuddering breath. 'Now, if you'll excuse me, I need to find my grandmother.'

The sooner she was able to return home and forget Fausto, she thought miserably, the better.

It had been a long eighteen hours. Long, aggravating, but so very worth it. Fausto glanced at the clock on the dashboard of his car—half past six on a beautiful spring evening. His eyes were gritty and his body ached. Last night he'd barely slept.

He'd checked with his staff to see if Liza had taken advantage of his offer of a private flight, only to learn that she had left with her grandmother in a cab before Roberto had been able to secure it. That knowledge had caused Fausto a ripple of unease, but he'd determinedly dismissed it. Liza had been in a rush to get back to her family. He understood her impatience; now he was in a rush to get back to her.

Unfortunately, finding her was not as simple as he hoped. He didn't have her telephone number, didn't know her address. The only thing he knew was her place of work, but it was evening and she wouldn't be there. He knew he could call Henry and ask for her address, but he was loath to put his godfather, Liza's employer, in such a position.

But he needed to see Liza. He'd left so abruptly in his determination to address the situation, and he feared she might have been besieged by doubts—although could either of them have any doubts after the incredible night they had shared? The aftershocks of emotion and pleasure were *still* rippling through him.

Even so, he needed to see her. Speak to her. *Hold her.* Once he did that, he was sure everything would be all right. It had to be.

He ended up calling Chaz. 'I need Jenna's number,' he stated brusquely.

'*Jenna?*'

'You have it still?'

'Of course I have it.' Something about Chaz's tone made Fausto ask, a little less brusquely, 'Why did you stop seeing her, by the way?'

Chaz was silent for a moment. 'I don't know,' he admitted.

'Was it because of what I said?'

'You told me to think carefully. I did.'

'So what were your concerns?'

Chaz sighed. 'I don't know. That she didn't feel for me as much as I felt for her? It was *frightening*, how much I felt. I backed away from it, I guess.'

Fausto knew all too well how that went. 'But you've been miserable without her,' he stated matter-of-factly. 'You should call her, Chaz.'

'It's been months—'

'So? Apologise. Grovel, if you have to.'

Chaz let out a choked laugh of disbelief. 'Are you, Fausto Danti, asking me to *grovel*?'

'I am.' Because, heaven knew, he might have to grovel too. He had left rather abruptly. 'If she's worth it and, judging from the way you've been these last few months, I think she is.'

'You really want me to call her?'

'Yes, but let me call her first.'

Jenna was as surprised to hear from him as Chaz had been when he'd asked for her number.

'You want Liza's number?'

'Preferably her address. I need to speak to her.'

'She's at home with us, here in Herefordshire.'

'May I have the address, please?'

Jenna hesitated.

'Please,' Fausto said quietly. 'I want to speak to her.' He paused as the words and their truth unfurled and grew inside him. Overwhelmed him. 'I need to tell her I love her.'

Jenna gave him the address.

* * *

It was a three-hour drive to the gracious Georgian house smothered with climbing roses in a pretty village over-looking rolling golden fields.

Fausto pulled into the drive and gazed at the house in bemused surprise—yes, the roof clearly needed re-pairing and it looked a little shabby and worn, but in a lovely, lovable way. The garden was full of bird feed-ers and ragged bunting, left over from a party perhaps, was strung along the gateposts.

He'd only just got out of the car when the front door was thrown open and Lindsay stood there, hands on her hips, eyes narrowed. Considering the disaster that had been so narrowly averted, she looked none the worse for wear.

'You look familiar,' she said.

'I met you with Chaz Bingham a few months ago,' he said, and she let out a squeal of recognition and delight.

'Oh, yes, you were so grumpy then.'

Faust gave a small smile in spite of himself. 'In-deed I was.'

'What on earth are you here for?' Lindsay demanded.

'Your sister, Liza.'

'Ooh!' The squeal was high-pitched enough to hurt Fausto's ears. '*Li-za!*' she yelled.

Fausto stepped inside the house. It was as lovably shabby on the inside as it was on the outside—all mis-matched chintz prints and comfortable sofas, as well as two shaggy golden retrievers who came up to him and immediately sprawled at his feet. Fausto was oddly enchanted by it all, by the homeliness of it, the com-fort and care, and most of all the love that radiated from every nook and cranny like a force field. And he'd thought Liza's family would reflect badly on *him*. The realisation, one he'd held in some dark corner of his heart up to even this moment, humbled him all the more.

Then Liza came into the hall—her face was pale, her curls riotous. She wore a loose green sundress and she looked absolutely wonderful.

'Fausto…' Her voice was faint. 'What are you doing here?'

'I needed to see you.'

'Why?'

'Yes, why?' Lindsay asked, clearly having no compunction about being a part of this conversation.

Fausto looked at Liza. 'May we speak in private?'

'Yes…the garden is probably the most private place.' She led him through the house, past her gawking mother, a smiling Jenna and another sister who had to be the bookish Marie. An older man with salt and pepper hair peeped out from a study and then quickly withdrew.

Liza brought him out to a small terrace in the back that overlooked a riotous garden of blowsy roses and bountiful wisteria.

'My father's pride and joy,' Liza said, nodding towards the many roses. 'That and the orchids, but those are in the greenhouse. Nothing like yours, of course. No rare varieties.' She glanced at the kitchen window, where four Benton women were openly staring, and then she nodded towards the lawn that wandered invitingly between trailing wisteria and overgrown rosebushes to a more private space.

'I don't know why you're here,' she said in a rather

wooden voice once they were free of the prying eyes and straining ears in the kitchen.

'I told you—to see you.'

'Yes, but why? Has…has something happened?'

Now that he had her here, had her attention, the words bottled up in his chest. He felt overcome with emotion, with certainty, and yet it was so hard to say it. As a boy he'd been taught all about pride and honour, dignity and respect. Not so much about vulnerability or love, yet those were what he felt—and needed—now.

'Fausto…?' The uncertainty in her voice made him ache.

'I love you.' It felt like something that could only be blurted, an admission straight from the gut—and the heart. Liza simply stared, so he decided to say it again. 'I love you. I want to spend the rest of my life with you.' It was like peeling back skin, offering his heart, still beating and raw, on a platter. It *hurt*. Then, to his amazement and horror, she slowly shook her head. This, then, was why he'd kept himself from saying the words for so long. The risk—the pain—were unbearable. 'You don't believe me?' he asked in a ragged voice.

'It's not that I don't believe you,' Liza said. 'Although, to be honest, I'm not sure if I do or not. It's that I'm not sure it matters.'

'What?' Fausto goggled at her, unable to keep himself from it—mouth open, eyes wide. 'What? How can it not? You told me you were holding out for love. That you wanted to marry a man who loved you—you, and only you. Well, I love you, Liza. I love you with my whole heart. My soul. My body. Everything. I've come to realise it—to revel in it!' He couldn't believe he was telling her so much, giving her so much, and yet she still seemed to be rejecting it. *Him*. He'd been so sure... again. How stupid could he be? How arrogant? Once again he'd thought she'd come to him with open arms.

'Yes, that's true,' Liza said after a moment, 'but Fausto, you don't *want* to love me.'

'I fought against it, that's true,' he said steadily. He would not shy away from his past sins. Perhaps now he still needed to atone for them. 'I did, because—'

'Because you didn't think I was *suitable*.' She said the words heavily rather than with scorn.

'No.'

Liza looked at him in surprise, and Fausto continued, this new level of vulnerability hurting him all the more. 'At least that was part of it, but really a small part. The truth was, I was afraid to love you. Afraid to give my heart.' He paused. 'Afraid to be hurt.'

'Like you were before.'

'Yes, although what I felt for her was nothing compared to this. Us.'

Her hazel gaze scanned his face. 'Your mother offered me money to go away.'

Fury streaked through him like a bolt of lightning. 'She's done that before.'

'Yes, she told me. And she told me that... Amy... took the money.'

Fausto's gut tightened at the memory. 'Yes.'

'I'm sorry. That must have been terrible.'

'It was a long time ago.'

'Yet these things still have the power to hurt us.' She paused, her gaze distant and troubled. 'I had a similar experience. I was hurt… Oh, it's a bit ridiculous because it never went anywhere. We only kissed.'

'What happened?' Fausto asked. He already despised whoever the man in question was.

'I met someone at uni. I thought he was interested in me. Well, he acted like he was. He flattered me…spent time with me. But then I discovered he was only interested in getting closer to Jenna.' She sighed, a wavery sound. 'He made that very clear.'

Bastard. 'I'm sorry, Liza.' Now he understood her insecurities, why she didn't believe he could love her. Her, and no other. 'Liza, I do love you,' he said in a low, insistent voice. 'Whatever happens between us, you need to know that. To believe it. I *want* to love you. Yes, I fought against it, and it was foolish of me. But I fought and I won. You won. And it is the sweetest victory, if you'll just…'

A small smile curved her lovely mouth. 'Love you back?'

'*Yes.*'

'I do love you.' Triumph rushed through him, tempered by her next words. 'But does it really change things, Fausto? I fought against loving you, just as you did with me. I can see that now. I was so angry, and that was in part because it felt as if you were making me look at my family differently, critically, and I hated that. I hated who I was becoming.'

'And I hate who I've *been.*'

'But what's changed, Fausto? Really?'

'I've changed,' he insisted. 'I've fallen in love for the very first time. I've seen a woman who is gracious and loving and kind, and I don't care if she was born a princess or a pauper. It doesn't matter.'

'It matters to your mother.'

His stomach tightened again at her despondent tone. 'My mother's concerns are not mine.'

'And yet you made it clear you wanted me gone.' She spoke matter-of-factly, yet he still heard her hurt.

'What?' Fausto stared at her in confusion. This was not part of the narrative that he understood. 'Why do you think that?'

'You left without even saying goodbye.'

'I was in a hurry—'

'Yes, I know, to do your own damage control. I do understand that.'

'My own...?' Now he could only look at her blankly. 'What is that supposed to mean?'

'Lindsay,' Liza said unhappily. 'I realised that if those photographs were published and our...association...was discovered it would reflect badly on you and your family. I'm sorry for that.'

'But the photos weren't published,' Fausto said slowly.

'No, amazingly they weren't. I don't know what happened. We weren't able to pay the money—'

'I paid the money,' Fausto said quietly, and Liza simply stared.

'You...' Then she nodded slowly. 'Because it would reflect badly on you, like I thought. I am sorry—'

'Liza, do you really think so little of me even now, after everything, that I would see off Jack Wickley simply because of how it affected me?' The pain in his voice was raw and audible, and he couldn't hide it.

She'd already told him she loved him and yet she still had these doubts?

'I don't understand...'

'I did it for you, because I love you! And for Lindsay, because she is young and everyone was young and foolish once, including me. And I did it because I could not bear to see Jack Wickley get away with one thing more. I paid him off and I had the photos destroyed, and I have gone to the police with the proof of his embezzling. I didn't do it before because my father wouldn't have wanted the shame on our company and name, which is another kind of damage pride does, but I realised Wickley can't get away with things—it only encourages him to do more, and to hurt more people.' He let out an exasperated, emotional breath. 'I did all that, but I *didn't* do any of it for some sort of *damage control*. I didn't even think about that. I couldn't care less about it now.'

Liza pressed her hands to her cheeks as tears filled her eyes. 'I don't know what you want me to say.'

'Say you love me again and that you'll marry me.'

Tears spilled down her cheeks. 'I'm not...'

'What?'

'Good enough,' she whispered. 'Special enough. Sophisticated enough...'

'You are all that and more, to me. And I will happily spend a lifetime proving it to you.'

'Even though I was so horrible to you?'

'You called me out. I deserved it.'

'You didn't...'

'Liza,' he said with a groan. 'I love you. You've said you love me. We can argue about the particulars, but right now I need you to kiss me.'

She laughed and then finally, wonderfully, she came into his arms and he let out a laugh of both relief and pure joy. She tilted her face up to his and he kissed her as he'd been aching to do.

'I do love you,' she said after a long moment. 'So much. I think I fell in love with you ages ago, and I fought it as much as you did, even though I didn't realise that was what I was doing at the time.'

'Then we've both had to surrender.'

'Yes.' She smiled, her face suffused with tenderness and love. 'Sweet, sweet surrender.'

Fausto kissed her again.

EPILOGUE

Seven months later

IT WAS THE wedding of the year. A Christmas wedding and, more than that, a double wedding—two gorgeous brides and two eminently eligible bachelors. The tabloids had a field day. It was on the cover of *You Too!* with an exclusive double page spread in the magazine.

There were four beautiful bridesmaids—Lindsay and Marie, Francesca, and Chaz's sister Kerry, who had thawed when she'd realised Fausto had never even looked at her that way. The ceremony was in the village church in Little Mayton, and the reception was in a luxury hotel nearby. Fausto had rented out the entire place for the occasion.

There would be another party to celebrate his and Liza's marriage in Italy, when they returned to Villa di Palmerno. Liza was going to work remotely for Henry as well as fulfil her duties as Contessa.

It was a fairy tale of epic proportions, and Liza felt as if she had to keep pinching herself. As she took a moment alone at the reception to watch all the gaiety, she did just that. A hard pinch on her upper arm, just to see.

'What are you doing?' Fausto asked, his voice laced with amusement as he came to stand beside her.

'Pinching myself. To make sure this is real.'

'Trust me, it's real.' He nodded towards the twelve-piece band that, on Lindsay's request, was starting a rendition of the Macarena, with Lindsay front and centre leading the dancing.

Liza let out a little muffled laugh. 'You don't mind?'

'Nope.' He slid his arms around her waist. 'Look at them all dancing.'

Liza glanced at her mother, who was giving it as much of her all as Lindsay was, and Jenna and Chaz, who were laughing and dancing, their arms around each other. Her father had even joined in and Henry and, amazingly, Viviana were both nodding along. Her mother-in-law had thawed towards her, if only just, but it was enough for Liza. She understood how hard it was to let go of preconceptions, of pride and prejudice.

'Happy?' Fausto asked as he nuzzled her hair, and she leaned against him as her thankfulness and joy overflowed.

'Yes,' she said, and turned her head to brush a kiss against his jaw. 'So, so happy.'

* * * * *

Love Harlequin romance?

DISCOVER.

Be the first to find out about promotions,
news and exclusive content!

f Facebook.com/HarlequinBooks

🐦 Twitter.com/HarlequinBooks

📷 Instagram.com/HarlequinBooks

📌 Pinterest.com/HarlequinBooks

You Tube YouTube.com/HarlequinBooks

ReaderService.com

EXPLORE.

Sign up for the Harlequin e-newsletter and
download a free book from any series at
TryHarlequin.com

CONNECT.

Join our Harlequin community to
share your thoughts and connect
with other romance readers!
Facebook.com/groups/HarlequinConnection

HSOCIAL2021